THE GHOST

A novel by

Sandra Brown Rarey

Mobjack Bay Publications

The characters and events in this book are fictitious. Any similarity to real persons, living or dead is coincidental and not intended by the author.

Copyright April 1, 2013 by Sandra Brown Rarey
Edition 2
Mobjack Bay Publications

CONTENTS

THE GHOST

A chilling and unexpected tale of deceit and desire.

Prologue

Elizabeth Barrett's house sat on the edge of a promontory that jutted over steep cliffs like a bony finger pointing at something beyond the foaming, angry seas; or, perhaps beckoning something unknown to come closer.

The house was nestled in deep cedars and green shadows that hid it from the rest of the world. It was her paradise on earth. She was at peace within its walls, her oft-broken heart safe and secure in the hands of Angus Aberdeen.

Elizabeth and Angus had lived together since the day she moved into the house. They'd had a perfect relationship for the past thirty-six months.

It didn't bother Elizabeth that Angus had been dead for well over a hundred years.

He never seemed to mind she was alive.

Peace and harmony reigned in the house at the end of Mulberry Drive…

Chapter <u>**1**</u>

Winter's early darkness was rapidly taking over the cold, damp day. It would be hours before the sun disappeared, but a three-quarter moon was already visible. Tall cedars rustled from the relentless wind that blew up the cliffs. Their shadows twisted and jerked like blue-gray dervishes on the snow and against the stone walls of Elizabeth Barrett's house.

Sometimes the wind soughed gently but today it was angry, bursting over the crest with a ferocity that left everything coated with salty overspray.

Elizabeth could taste it in the air. She pushed at the heavy oak door until it gave with a groan. It needed to be replaced but that would be expensive. Besides, it gave her home a touch of outdated charm. As did everything else about it, she thought, tossing her keys into a copper pot on the sideboard in her entry hall.

She removed yesterday's mail from the pot and added it to the stash in her hand. Slipping out of her boots, she curled her toes into the worn oriental runner. A shiver of delight had her hugging herself and smiling. She was home. She loved the old monstrosity of a house with its turrets and buttresses as much as her friends and co-workers loved their own suburban ranchers and cul-de-sac colonials.

She hung her scarf and coat on the hall tree and glanced in the mirror above the sideboard. Her hair was a mess. It trailed across her wind-chapped cheeks. She combed it with her fingers. Her cold nose was red, but her mouth was smiling and her eyes sparkled. "Angus," she whispered. "I'm home."

The aroma of apple pie crept in from the kitchen. The scent conjured up images of her family when she was young, sitting around the table on frigid winter evenings like this one. She could almost see her mother's face. Angus seemed to know exactly what memories she held dear, and the exact aromas to bring them to life.

"Mmmm," she said. "That smells great! Thank you." She went into the parlor where the stained-glass chandelier glowed like a kaleidoscope held to the sun. Angus turned it on every evening for her. A fire burned crackling hot in the fireplace. She lingered there, absorbing the warmth. Strains of "Claire De Lune" drifted in from the formal living room.

"Work was a bear today. I'm exhausted." She padded into the kitchen. The booming of the surf was louder in here. It made a perfect harmony with the music Angus had so thoughtfully provided.

Candlelight flickered off the walls and the pressed tin ceiling. She wondered, yet again, where Angus got his endless supply of candles. She sometimes brought home scented tapers and pillars but he never lit them for her. As a joke, she'd once bought a candle from the 75% off Halloween aisle at the drugstore. It was an image of Casper, The Friendly Ghost.

She thought it was funny. Angus had not. She found the decapitated candle three days later in the crisper of her refrigerator. Apparently Angus had no sense of humor.

Elizabeth set the bills and junk mail on the counter after thumbing through them to see if her mother had written. She hadn't, and there was a measure of relief that she wouldn't have to add another letter to the pile of those unread. The letters were mostly pleas for information and demands for communication. Her mother didn't understand Elizabeth's need for solitude. She certainly would never understand her infatuation with a ghost.

She fished a molasses cookie from a glass canister. "Angela didn't come in today," she said. The cookie was gone in three bites and only served to make her hungrier. "Christy took over for her, but there were so many claims from the storm we couldn't process them all. And, as usual, there were dozens of people trying to buy coverage after the fact."

The January nor'easter had slammed into New England over the weekend, downing trees, snapping power lines and dumping two feet of snow on the town of Midville.

Elizabeth emptied a can of chicken soup into a bowl. Angus was probably bored with her chatter about her co-workers at the insurance agency--if spirits could get bored. But this was part of their daily routine. He certainly couldn't add to the conversation. "Jody showed up wearing sunglasses," she continued aloud. "She said the snow hurt her eyes but she never took them off. I think she had been crying. The other girls speculated about it all day."

Bypassing the massive black gas stove that dominated one side of the kitchen, she set her soup in the microwave, all the while wishing Angus had the ability to really cook his wonderful concoctions. A piece of that apple pie would taste delicious right now. Sometimes his fragrances set up a real hunger in her belly. Perhaps she should buy him a cook book.

The scent of clove and cinnamon disappeared. Elizabeth sighed with regret. "I'm sorry," she said. "I wasn't complaining. I appreciate all you do for me, Angus,

I really do." She loved Angus. She loved living with the presence of a ghost whose primary reason for existence seemed to be to keep her happy. What she didn't love was his ability to read her mind.

He apparently wasn't in a forgiving mood. Her home remained aroma free. She crushed a handful of saltines into the soup and carried it to the table with a glass of Riesling. On the way, she pushed the top button of a wall switch. A burst of light from the bulbs overhead dispelled the gloom. Sitting on an old wooden chair, she curled her bare toes on the rung and picked up her glass.

The candles he'd lit went out with a snap, leaving smoky tendrils dancing in the air like disconnected cobwebs.

"Fine, you can go off and pout. I'll have supper by myself." She carried her soup and wine to her bedroom and absentmindedly ate while answering long overdue emails on her laptop. Angus wasn't going to ruin her evening with his childish behavior.

Truth was, although he provided the comfort and security of a dear friend, there were times she wanted to be alone. Not often, and not for long. But she wondered if she didn't occasionally think of things that would send Angus off in a huff so she didn't feel compelled to converse with thin air. One-sided conversations were unsatisfying, and talking to him with her mind felt too much like praying.

She had no idea where he went when he left her. Angus had lived in this house much longer than she; he must have his own places of comfort.

Elizabeth rinsed her bowl and glass in the bathroom sink and turned them upside down on a hand towel. She flipped the light switch and felt her way through the dark to her high, old four-poster bed. While she waited for sleep, she wondered why she was content with so little.

She had friends at work and email buddies, but they seldom intruded into her personal space. She liked it like that. She admittedly missed her mother, but not her tearful interrogations and smothering concern.

She seldom saw her parents. To be honest, that was her fault. They had tried to maintain ties with her as each of her paramours left her more fragile and damaged. Their well-meaning interference was like a reprimand, a litany of her wrong choices. She wouldn't listen to their advice and she refused to live her life the way they thought she should, so she'd moved to New England and built her cocoon. Except for her mother's weekly letters, communication with them had diminished to a comfortable level and they had stopped pleading to visit.

The truth was she didn't want to share her home, or her time in it with anyone. She especially didn't want to share Angus. Or be subjected to the opinions of those who might disapprove. She knew he had been a spirit for well over a hundred years. Somehow he had infused that knowledge in her. Or had he? Was that something her imagination had drummed up in a need to know him better? Was it wishful thinking? Old ghosts were romantic.

New ghosts were simply frightening.

As she snuggled in bed awaiting sleep, she was ambushed by an unwelcome need for more. How would his arms feel around her? She imagined his caresses and pretended he was there in the four-poster with her. She imagined his presence pressing her into the mattress. She could almost feel his breath on her shoulders, his lips brushing across her own.

Her chest rose and fell. Her skin pebbled, raising the fine hairs on her arms. She ran her hands over her hot, dry skin. How would she feel to Angus? Her nipples hardened. Her breasts swelled. The sensations were exquisite, more so because they were unreal.

Try as she might, she couldn't capture and hold the feelings racking her. She would soon return to reality because she had no choice. Her ghost was not in bed with her. He would never join her there except in her dreams. Perhaps that was for the best. A man who couldn't touch you couldn't leave bruises.

Cold comfort that was.

Chapter 2

Monday was President's Day. It was also Elizabeth's birthday and she was looking forward to a quiet, special evening. Most insurance agencies were closed, along with government offices. But Mr. Clark believed holiday sales brought folks out to shop and he expected a certain percentage would drop into the office to apply for insurance while they were out loading up on electronics and groceries.

The only drop-in customers today had been there to complain about rejected claims or to make late payments which entailed a lot of reinstatement paperwork.

Elizabeth finished up for the day and shut down her computer. A Christmas cactus sat on her desk beside a framed photo of her parents taken almost ten years ago. She dumped the remainder of her bottled water over the dusty leaves. She might come in a few minutes early tomorrow and give the plant a bath.

But for now, she was anxious to be home. If only there was a way to get there without driving in the icy slush while waiting for her car to warm up and the windows to defrost. Wrapping her scarf around her neck, she shrugged into her old down-filled jacket. It wasn't a fashion statement, but it was the warmest coat she'd ever owned.

Angela and Christy hovered, apparently in no more hurry to go out into the cold and wet than she was. "See you tomorrow," she murmured distractedly, reaching for her boots.

"Wait," Christy said. "Don't put those on yet. We have a surprise for you."

Her stomach rolled. She hated surprises that focused on her. They made her feel awkward and self-conscious. "I can't wear my boots for a surprise?"

"Not where we are going." Christy flashed an expectant grin and waved a pink envelope in front of her. "Did you think we forgot your birthday?"

"Yes, I did." Elizabeth took the card and slid her finger beneath the flap. The card opened to a view of a cartoon couple in a torrid clench. *May your wildest dreams come true!* it read. She forced a chuckle. She hadn't mentioned her birthday and had assumed no one remembered. "Thanks."

"Happy birthday, honey." Angela gave her a hug. "We're going to celebrate. You wouldn't let us have a party for you last year, so this year we didn't ask. We're taking you to Damon's Pub."

"Now? But I have to—" Elizabeth turned away so Angela couldn't see her face flame. She'd been out of sorts for days, feeling slightly discontented. That had changed this morning when she'd awakened to the aroma of birthday cake. It had enveloped her like a cloud of cotton candy, making her feel like a child again. Angus had given her a wonderful gift. She'd thought about him all day and couldn't wait to see what else he had planned.

Her friends would think she was certifiable if she told them she lived with a ghost who would expect her to spend her birthday with him. He would be waiting for her. "I have to go home first."

Angela took a stance and folded her arms. "We've planned this for a week. Now you're trying to come up with an excuse not to go."

The reproach made her feel guilty. "No, I'm not." She wouldn't deliberately hurt her friends' feelings. She had to go, or admit things they wouldn't comprehend. She looked down on her white cotton blouse and basic black slacks. "I was going to say I wanted to change my clothes, but I'm okay in this."

"You look fine," Christy said. "We're going as we are. And we really do have a surprise waiting."

"Just let me run to the bathroom and tidy up a bit."

"We'll wait out front."

"I'll only be a minute," she said, biting her lower lip. It seemed the events of the rest of the day were out of her control and she would have to make the best of it.

Elizabeth washed her hands and checked her reflection. Of course they were going as they were. Angela always wore sleek, sexy outfits with tight skirts and low necklines. Her blonde, chopped hair was meant to be worn messy. And Christy was flash and fire, a stunning gypsy who dressed in Bohemian clothes that few women could wear well.

Brushing her brown hair into a smooth waterfall, Elizabeth tucked one side behind her ear, exposing a gold loop. She reapplied the pale coral lipstick she'd managed to chew off during the day, and undid the top button of her blouse. Not half bad, she thought, wondering if Angus would approve.

Angus. Uneasiness set up in her belly. How would she explain this to him? And how would he react?

She bundled back into her old coat and ruefully eyed her boots. They looked warm and comfortable, but Christy was right. They were not meant for clubbing. She shoved them beneath her desk. Her feet would freeze on the drive home tonight.

She left the building to find Angela and Christy waiting at the curb. They stood next to a man in a crisp gray uniform. Behind them a limo was parked against an embankment of snow that was crusted over with dirt and sand. The girls began to sing, "Happy Birthday to You."

"Oh, my gosh!" She clapped her hands and laughed. This might be fun, if she could get past the nagging guilt.

"Happy birthday, Miss," the driver said, doffing his hat. He opened the rear door and took her elbow, guiding her over the snow and into the coffin-like interior of the vehicle.

Her gasp of delight turned into a choked protest when a man in a tuxedo gathered her onto his lap. Her purse slid to the floor. His hands slid around her waist. She had a brief impression of dark skin and felt hard muscles through the goose down jacket as her friends piled in behind her.

"Liz, this is Steele. He's a dancer at Midnight Madness."

"It's nice to meet you, Steele." A dancer? More than likely he was a male stripper. She swallowed a snort of amusement when he growled in her ear. Was that supposed to be sexy? He tightened his grip and nuzzled her neck. His breath was hot beneath her earring. She leaned forward, away from him. Slowly unzipping her jacket, he slid it down her arms and held her captive for another assault on her neck.

She cringed. Her shoulders tightened. Her level of

discomfort rose. There was too much about his antics that smacked of domination. She pulled her arms free of the jacket.

Steele tossed it on the floor next to her purse. The girls giggled while she tried to be a good sport.

Steele was obviously enjoying himself. He suddenly whisked off his tuxedo jacket and left her leaning into bare flesh. She jerked away. "If you remove one more piece of clothing, yours or mine, I'll jump out of this limo, moving or not." She was serious but kept her tone light. She didn't want to offend him.

They all laughed as if she'd made a joke.

She maneuvered off him and squirmed between the girls.

Angela shrugged out of her coat and took her place.

Christy handed her a cocktail in a bottle.

The vodka drink bubbled with a diffusion of peach and mango. It tickled her nose and helped her relax. The more she sipped, the funnier Steele's antics became. By the time they arrived at Damon's, he had Angela giving him a silly lap dance. Thank goodness they had exchanged places.

When the chauffer pulled up in front of the club, she struggled back into her jacket. She still held the empty cocktail bottle. She wouldn't leave it on the floor for someone else to pick up, so she slipped it into her coat pocket.

Steele apparently had fulfilled his purpose, as he

stayed behind when they slid out of the limo.

Harsh rock music blasted through the pub and seemed to vibrate through the thick stucco walls. The sidewalk was littered with people, laughing and talking loudly. Some stood in groups; some leaned against the building, smoking, changing color with the flashing neon sign. A stale, smoky stench spilled from the open door.

Inside there was standing room only. Christy disappeared for a few minutes. She came back and handed Elizabeth a drink. "This is an Appletini."

"What?" Elizabeth clutched it to her chest with both hands. She could hardly hear Christy. The roar of voices and music shot a pain between her eyes. It had been a long time since she had been in a club. It was exciting and a little nerve-wracking.

"Appletini. Taste it. And for goodness sake, take that jacket off. You look like the Pillsbury Doughboy."

She giggled, but she was embarrassed. She took it off and tucked it under her arm. It was like carrying a pillow.

"Are you going to drink that? I can get you something else if you would rather."

Elizabeth sniffed her drink and then took a tentative sip. "Wow. No, this is great! Thanks."

"The band is Novacula," Angela shouted. "They're from Niagara Falls. Let's get closer."

Someone jostled her, spilling his drink on her shoe. She almost felt assaulted when he shoved past, his clothes dragging against hers. "It's too crowded," she protested.

"I'd rather stay by the bar. Maybe we'll get lucky and find some empty stools."

Christy scowled as they worked their way away from the band.

"Happy birthday to Elizabeth Barrett," the lead singer announced. The pub patrons ignored the announcement. Her friends clapped, whistled and pointed at her.

Embarrassed, she ducked her head.

"That's why we wanted to get closer," Christy shouted.

"I'm sorry." She was spoiling their good intentions. "I really am. Do you want to go back? I don't mind."

"It is okay, Liz," Angela said. "We're here to have a good time."

Elizabeth smiled brightly and gulped her drink. It left an aftertaste that reminded her of Angus's apple pie scent. She set her empty glass on the bar. "I'd like another, please, and drinks for them, too." She handed the bartender two twenty-dollar bills.

"Put your money away," Christy said. "This is our gift to you."

"Thanks." She took a long, slow drink of the Appletini. It went down like silk. "These are delicious."

The man next to her vacated his bar stool. She slid her jacket over the seat but remained standing.

"We'll be right back," Christy called behind her as she and Angela disappeared into the crowd.

Time slid by until the band went on break. Their

abrasive noise was replaced by canned classical rock. Elizabeth leaned on the bar, her back to the room, watching the gaiety unfold through the wall-length mirror as she sang to, 'Fat Bottom Girls'. Were they simply going to leave her there for the bartender to babysit? Feeling abandoned and pathetic she ordered another Appletini and polished it off in a couple of gulps.

Chapter 3

The band started up again. Elizabeth's pulse accelerated to the pull of the live music.

A few minutes later Christy returned, all out of breath. Her eyes sparkled. Her hair clung damply to her cheek.

"Where were you?" Elizabeth asked.

"I was dancing with Angela. But this guy kept cutting in. You should get out there and have fun! Come on, dance with me."

"Maybe in a minute," Elizabeth said. She was drinking too much, but she didn't object when Christy ordered her another drink. They tasted like liquid dessert. She smiled when she remembered how Angus had sulked when she'd wished he could cook. It was his fault she craved the flavor of apple pie.

"Would you like to dance?"

Elizabeth turned to the voice behind her. The man's eyes sparkled good-naturedly. For a moment, her heart raced with anticipation. Her muscles tightened, ready to move to the music of Journey. But her momentary flash of interest fled. The confidence she had rebuilt since coming to Midville shriveled. "I'm sorry. I don't know how."

"I'll teach you."

"Really, I have no sense of rhythm."

"No problem. You don't have to move much. I just put my hands here . . ." He put a hand on her shoulder and the other on her hip. "Take a step or two, sway a littl and the next thing you know, we'll be dancing."

"I'm sorry." She pulled away, turned her back to him and hitched herself onto the stool. She'd lied. She loved to dance, but her social skills had rusted long ago. She didn't know how to make casual conversation anymore. She would make a fool of herself. He would be sorry he asked her.

Still, she almost gasped in protest when the interest slid from his expression.

She'd been touched by two mortal men in the past hour. Touched and stroked by warm, human hands for the first time in years. The sensations brought back the dissatisfaction she had been fighting for a week. And now she was in a bad mood.

"It's been almost four years," Christy said as the man left Elizabeth and approached another woman. "You're never going to get on with your life if you don't get over Bobby."

"It's a little hard to get over the man who broke your arm. And Jason, who had a wife I knew nothing about; and Dean, who drank himself into oblivion every chance he got."

"Where did that come from?" Angela looked at Elizabeth's glass. "How many of those have you had?"

Elizabeth shrugged. "Four."

Angela glanced over her shoulder at Christy. Her mouth flattened. "There's a lot of booze in those drinks. Maybe you should get up and move around a little."

"I'm fine. I want to stay right here. It's just that you two make it look so easy, going from one man to another."

"That's not fair," Christy huffed. "I haven't spoken to a single guy yet, and, if I do, so what? I'm unattached. So are you."

"I didn't mean tonight. I meant in general. And it wasn't an insult. I envy your romances. You seem to have so much fun."

"You could too if you'd loosen up."

"Christy's right," Angela said. "This place is full of single guys. Flirt a little. Pick someone up for a few hours."

"I don't think so. I'm not interested in a casual

encounter." She drained her glass, loving the feel of the smooth, spicy liquid as it slid down her throat. "But I think I'm in love with these," she said, lifting the empty glass in an unsteady toast. She wanted long-term love. She wanted kindness and respect, like her father gave her mother. The conversation was becoming uncomfortable but Elizabeth didn't know how to end it.

"There's nothing wrong with having fun while you're young." Christy said.

"I wouldn't know. I haven't had much fun in my relationships."

"So you're going to give up?"

"No. I'm just not ready to jump back into dating. I will, eventually, because I would like to get married someday." There. She'd said it. The wish was always there, but she'd kept it buried. Angus was too insightful.

"So would I," Angela said, making them all laugh. She had been engaged twice in the past three years and got cold feet both times. Since then several men had drifted in and out of her life.

"Me, too," Christy said. "Next time someone proposes to you, just do the guy a favor. Let him down gently and then send him my way."

"Or mine," Elizabeth said with a chuckle. What was it, she wondered, that scared Angela about commitment? Both of her ex-fiancés were really nice guys.

She, herself was willing to commit to a forever relationship with the right person. It was the men in her life that had issues with brutality and fidelity and so many other things. "I'm on the lookout for a good man, but I can't find one." She certainly wouldn't find one in this nightclub where men looked at women like they were displays in a vending machine.

Thank goodness her ghost didn't hear that. He would make her life miserable. He might even leave her. She couldn't bear that. "Maybe it's me. Maybe I have a knack for choosing the wrong men." She handed the bartender her empty glass. He handed her a full one. She sipped this one slowly. "Or maybe there is no such thing as a decent man."

"The world is full of decent men," Christy said. "I know I'll find someone wonderful. In the meantime, I intend to have fun with the bad boys."

"You mean the liars, the drunks, the abusers?"

"What's wrong with you?" Angela snapped. "We brought you here to celebrate and you're spoiling the evening."

What was wrong with her? Her friends had gone through a lot of trouble and expense to show her a good time. She was behaving badly and she knew it. "I'm sorry. Let's not talk about this anymore."

Angela and Christy seemed more than happy to oblige. They disappeared into the crowd, leaving her on the verge of tears.

Feeling sorry for herself, she ruthlessly tamped down the guilt she felt for her ungrateful, belligerent behavior.

She still felt bad about leaving Angus alone on a night that was special.

A burst of laughter drew her attention. At the end of the bar a woman slipped from the grasp of one man only to be manhandled by another. Elizabeth swallowed a breath of panic as old feelings came to the surface. Laughing, the woman pulled away from both. She slid herself onto the lap of a third. Her actions were sensual and deliberate. She didn't appear to be at all frightened to have three strong, vital young men closing in on her with lusty intent.

What must that feel like? Elizabeth finished her fifth Appletini and closed her eyes. She tried to imagine flirting with several men at once. Angus would surely make her life a misery if he were here to read her thoughts. Ghostly retribution. A soft laugh escaped. What would that consist of? Would he conjure the fragrances of fire and brimstone instead of lavender? Light her house on fire instead of his endless supply of candles? Her head lolled back.

"Elizabeth!"

The stool spun and she almost lost her balance. "What?" Christy and Angela were staring at her. They'd each brought back a partner. There was another man with them, a handsome stranger who was clearly meant for her.

"Are you okay?" Angela asked.

"I don't think the Appletinis are settling well. I feel a little sick to my stomach."

"Have a glass of mineral water," Angela suggested with an accusing glance at Christy.

Elizabeth pressed her hands against the bulky scarf knotted on her chest. "No. No mineral water. I have to get out of here. Can you have the bartender call me a cab?"

"The limo will be here at midnight to take us back to the agency to pick up our cars," Christy said. "It's twenty after ten now. You can wait a little while, can't you? There's someone we want you to meet."

They had been here over three hours. Angus must be worried. A sense of urgency propelled her off the barstool onto unsteady feet. "I'm not feeling well. Please, just get me a taxi."

"I don't believe this." Christy sounded exasperated. She fisted her hands on her hips. "I'm not ready to leave. I'm having a good time."

"I'm not ready to leave, either." Angela leaned into her new escort who hooked an arm around her neck, drawing her closer.

"I didn't ask you to. You both stay and take the limo." She slipped into her jacket and hooked her purse strap over her shoulder.

"If you insist." Angela motioned the bartender. "Can you call a taxi for her?" She gave Elizabeth a squeeze. "Happy birthday, lightweight," she said with a smile. "Take the cab straight home. Leave your car at work. I'll pick you up in the morning."

"You don't have to do that. I'll just take a cab to work."

"Okay. But, call me if you change your mind. It's no

problem to come get you."

Elizabeth dared a glance at the man she was supposed to meet. He had his attention on another woman. Too bad. She could use a strong arm to escort her outside, and his looked perfect for the job.

Angela and Christy refused to leave her until they were certain a taxi was on the way. They moved closer to the entrance. When she heard a short honk through the open door she wobbled outside. Her stomach rolled. She wasn't drunk, but she definitely wasn't sober. It was going to be an interesting night when she got home.

Chapter 4

Elizabeth groped her way through the dark house towards her kitchen. She was hungry. Her head hurt. Her legs felt like rubber. She maneuvered with the care of an invalid, bracing against furniture and the walls.

There was no lovely aroma teasing her. No Debussy to wash her mind of the abrasive club music. Rays from the full moon fractured on the metal grillwork of the windows in the parlor. They splattered the room with crazy patterns. There was no other light.

"Angus. I want my birthday cake," she called. Her

slightly slurred demand echoed back to her. When it dissipated, the only response was the sound of the sea far below the cliff upon which her house was built.

She loved that sound. She had grown so accustomed to the sea she knew without a doubt she could never live away from here. On evenings like tonight, when Angus deserted her, its crashing, boiling hiss kept the loneliness at bay.

Where was he?

Feeling abandoned and sorry for herself, she forgot about food. She curled in a chair by the cold fireplace. Reliving the evening, she decided her musings at Damon's had been alcohol-fueled and foolish. Now that she was home safe and sound, she realized she didn't need a mortal man. She had no right to those desires. She'd made her choice three years ago when she had moved into this house and melted into the comfortable, secure existence of living with Angus. Angus cherished her. Angus was safe. He would never harm her or lie to her. He kept her from repeating her self-destructive mistakes. Angus was the perfect man with whom to spend eternity.

She believed she held the same vital importance to Angus as he did to her. She felt his affection when she came home to glowing candles and soft music. He spoke to her heart when the fragrance of flowers filled the rooms and bone-deep warmth from the fireplace dispelled winter's chill.

It was obvious he cared nothing for her comfort

tonight.

Shivering, she glanced at the stack of firewood on the hearth. Three years had passed and she hadn't learned to start a fire. Three years since her aunt and uncle had been killed in a terrible accident. This house had been theirs. Now it was hers. And she was cold.

She stacked three poplar logs in a triangle and thought about the matches in a drawer in the kitchen. She waived her hands at the fireplace. "Abracadabra." Her laugh was a puff of air that ended with a snort. "Well, so much for my non-existent magical fire-starting ability." She hugged herself and stared at the logs. Angus never needed wood for his flames. "You're no gentleman," she muttered. She might have been sorry for the complaint if she thought he was near.

Was he absent merely because she was late, or because he knew she'd had too much to drink? Although she couldn't feel his presence, she tried to block images of Steele from her mind. He was an experience she didn't want to share with Angus. Her wayward thoughts in the bar had to be suppressed, too. She certainly didn't want him to sense the wildness deep inside her a few drinks had brought out.

"I need you." She waited for the thrilling sensation that would tell her he was present. It didn't come. "Love is constant, Angus. And it is forgiving. If I hurt you, I'm sorry. It was truly unavoidable. No matter what, you should be here for me." She'd never before spoken of love to him. Perhaps it was time.

Perhaps not, since he remained aloof.

The matchbox was empty. She'd used the matches up on that old gas stove. There was nothing to do but go to bed and wait for morning.

She fell asleep immediately and dreamed of being beaten, and then left in a shack set on fire by a mob. She whimpered and feverishly tossed and turned. The horrible nightmare brought her to the surface over and over. She could hear her own terrified screams and smell her own burnt flesh.

As she slept, her sheets curled at the corners, turning black and scorched.

The morning sun's rays stabbed her poor brain through her closed eyelids. She opened them one at a time and sat up in bed. Her mouth tasted like dirty laundry. Her head hurt. Her stomach ached. She was never going to overindulge in alcohol again.

She showered and then bundled up in an oversized flannel bathrobe and went downstairs to turn the thermostat up. She should have done this before she showered. It was freezing.

The ancient furnace grumbled from below. It reminded her of Steele's lusty growl. She laughed, and then clutched her head. Aspirin. She needed aspirin. She searched her cupboards and found nothing. The bottle had always been in her spice cabinet and now, when she needed it, it was gone.

Sitting with her head in her hands, waiting for the coffee maker to spit out a pot of coffee, she remembered her car was at work. A quick glance told her it was almost 8:00. She was running late, certainly too late to call Angela. She would have to call a taxi like she'd planned. She had no idea what she was going to wear to work. Her hair was wet. There was no time to blow dry and style it.

She had taken two sick days off since she started working at the agency, and no personal time. What would it hurt to call in sick? Mr. Clark would understand. And her work load was caught up.

She made up her mind, grabbed a cup of coffee and went upstairs where she dressed in her warm sweatshirt and pants. The coffee settled her stomach. If only she could get rid of the headache, she might enjoy her time off.

She stripped the damp, wrinkled sheets from her bed. Uncovering the charred edges of the fabric, she gasped with dismay. *What on earth?* She fingered the crispy edges of the cotton. An acrid smell turned her stomach. No wonder she had dreamed of burning. The odor must have penetrated her sleep. She'd just washed her bedding three days ago and had noticed no problem with her dryer. But then, as usual, she'd been focused on grabbing the laundry and leaving the dank cellar with its creepy shadows as soon as possible. She felt like she was buried alive when she was down there.

Why hadn't she noticed the charring when she had

made the bed? She balled the stinking sheets and set them on the balcony outside the leaded glass doors beside her bed. Ice coated the balustrade. A sharp wind blew past her, whipping her curtains and filling her bedroom. She dropped the ball of bedding and slammed the doors shut. Tiny chips of sleet drummed against the glass. It was like a blizzard out there. She was glad she had decided to stay home.

The sheets would get washed later and then hung in that musty old basement to dry. They would smell of the cellar, but still, a repairman would have to look at the dryer before she would use it again. It could have set her house on fire.

Blow-drying her hair, she pulled it into a pony tail. She pulled on a sweatshirt, slid into a pair of sweat pants and found her warm, worn Ugg slippers under the bed.

She went downstairs and phoned the office at 8:45. Mr. Clark sounded genuinely sympathetic, which took away her anxiety about making the last minute call. She had the day to herself.

She poured another cup of coffee. With the first sip, the band on her pony tail snapped. Her hair electrified. It flew into a static halo around her face, tickling her forehead and neck. With the second sip, a sensation of warm cream spread down her body beneath her clothes. The coffee suddenly smelled like chocolate. Her tension dissolved. Her muscles went lax. The cup almost slipped from her fingers.

The clanking, groaning furnace was drowned out by the strains of harps and flutes. The thrilling notes made her think of spring. The room flared with heat that had her kicking off her slippers. She clutched her coffee to her chest and laughed out loud from joy and relief. Angus had forgiven her.

Chapter **5**

The deep clang of door chimes jolted her. Elizabeth splashed coffee on her sweatshirt. She brushed the drops off, irritated to have been interrupted. No one had twisted that bell handle since she'd moved in. "I'm sorry, Angus. I'll be right back." She set her cup down and hooked her fingers in her slippers, carrying them into the front hall.

The chimes sounded again. She rushed through the parlor, flicking the chandelier on as she passed. In the entry hall she stepped on something sharp. Crying out in pain, she dropped her slippers. Broken glass was scattered on the hall runner. It was the cocktail bottle. It must have fallen out of her jacket pocket last night. It had shattered as if the floor was made of concrete instead of carpet. How had she missed stepping on it this morning?

A third chime rolled into a fourth as she pushed the broken bottle and glass shards to the side with her bare foot and peered through the viewer. It was very early, and visitors seldom came to this end of her secluded street.

A stranger's distorted features filled her vision. Annoyed and a little unnerved, she turned the lock and tugged at the heavy door. It opened with a protesting creak.

The thought she might be in danger came too late when the stranger stomped the snow from his boots and stepped across her threshold before she had the chance to say anything.

Elizabeth's heart raced. Her muscles tensed to run. Was there something within reach she could use as a weapon? She should have thought twice before opening the door. *Angus? Are you still here?*

The stranger was bundled against the January weather. The collar of his long coat was turned up against his jaws. He hunched into it. His mouth was a flat line. A hat rode low on his head, shadowing the rest of his expression. He looked menacing, like a serial killer.

Was this going to be her last day on earth? Could she reach the broken bottle before he grabbed her? She stepped back, refusing to cry out when she realized there was a sliver of glass in her foot. This was the first time she had ever been fearful in her isolation. If she made it through the day she was going to buy a gun, a small pistol just in case. The thought made her angry. This person had no right coming here and scaring her in her own home.

When she stepped back, he stepped back, too. She released a breath she didn't know she'd been holding. The little bit of distance between them gave her the courage to straighten her spine and glare at him. How dare he enter her home without permission? "Excuse me? Can I help you?" She kept her tone hard and unfriendly and jutted her chin, hoping he couldn't see it wobble.

He brushed snowflakes off his sleeve, his gaze following their drift to the broken glass on the carpet.

She reflexively looked down, too. There were fresh blood stains on the carpet.

"Ma'am," he said as he raised his hand.

Elizabeth flinched, and then felt foolish when he removed his hat.

His hair was long. It touched his shoulders and was disheveled enough to make him look appealing. His eyes were starkly blue in a face white from cold. They held a hint of pleading.

It was the expression in those eyes that relaxed her fear. They radiated benevolence. So did his slight smile. Not that she was going to let down her guard, but there was no threat in his demeanor--if she could dismiss the fact that he was in her hallway without invitation.

She glanced at the flurries swirling in the wind off her porch. A row of cedars curved across her lawn, casting long shadows and blocking the rest of the world from view. There was no car parked within her vision. Had he walked down that long, lonely road?

"Are you selling something?" She touched her hair. If he was a salesman, she would most likely wind up owning whatever it was he sold.

"I'm Duncan Munroe," he said. "I hope you can help me. I've come a long way."

He unbuttoned his coat as if he intended to stay and what little trust his expression had inspired fled right out the door. "Don't take your coat off!" The words were sharp and high. She took another step back, this time anticipating the stabbing pain in her foot. "What do you want, Mr. Munroe?"

"I'm looking for someone, Miss Barrett. I think he might live here."

The fact he knew her name was ominous. "If you know who I am, you must know I--" She'd almost admitted she lived alone. "Whoever you're looking for doesn't live here. I'm sorry."

"I believe he does. His name is Angus Aberdeen."

The blood drained from her face. Shaken, she braced herself with a hand on the wall. No one knew about Angus. No one.

"I've never heard of him," she said. "I'm sorry, but you have to leave."

He shivered and pulled his collar higher. "I can't do that, ma'am. Not until I talk to you. It really is very cold out there and I would like to come in."

"This is my home. I'm telling you to leave." She immediately regretted her sharp tone. She didn't want to anger him. "Please," she said softly, and then hoped he wouldn't take her plea as vulnerability. Acting with much more bravery than she felt, Elizabeth stepped toward him and tried to move him back out the door with the force of her presence.

He refused to budge. "I really need a moment of your time, Miss Barrett. I'll be quick, and then I will let you get on with your day."

How dare he? She wanted to forcefully shove him away, but was leery of touching him. She was at his mercy if he'd come to do her harm, but she wouldn't show her fear. She'd learned from experience that just fanned the flames of a bad temper. "If you won't leave," she said, "I will call the police." Unfortunately she'd left her cell phone charging in the kitchen.

"There's no need for that. I will be gone as soon as I ask you a few questions," he said. "I assure you, you have nothing to fear from me."

"What questions? Are you doing a survey? Are you an investigator?"

"I'm neither. I'm a simple man looking for answers, and hoping I can do you a service."

A service. So he was a salesman-a pushy one. That

explained how he knew about Angus. Whatever solicitation list he had gotten his leads from must be way out of date. If only he knew he came to pitch his product to a man who had been dead for a long time.

She might have felt sorry for him, making a living like this. However, his hat looked like handmade felt and his coat was Burberry if she wasn't mistaken. There was a similar one in her uncle's closet upstairs.

He apparently wasn't going to leave until he'd said his piece. He certainly was insistent, but then again he would have to be to compete in this age of Internet sales and phone solicitation. There was no case in his hand, so he wasn't selling perfumes or cosmetics. His questions were probably going to involve her satisfaction with her vacuum cleaner, if they still sold them door-to-door.

But he had asked for Angus. Maybe he was selling insurance.

"Hurry up. Say what you have to say," she snapped. If he thought for one minute she was going to invite him into the house he was mistaken. They would stay right here in the entry and the door would remain open even though there wasn't another person within a quarter mile.

He glanced down at the broken glass, then at her feet. "As I said, I'm looking for Angus Aberdeen."

That didn't sound like a sales pitch. She flinched as she slid into her slippers. Her foot was bloody and hurt like hell. Where on earth was Angus? Could he help her if she needed him? "So you said. I live here with my brothers.

We've never heard of the person you're looking for."

A quirk of his lips told her he most likely knew that was a lie. She flushed with alarm, suddenly suspecting this man knew more about her than her name. "Why are you looking for this Angus person?"

"He murdered my wife."

Chapter 6

"Thank you."

"It was just scrambled eggs and toast, but you're certainly welcome," Elizabeth said. Duncan Monroe had shared her breakfast and no longer seemed like a sinister stranger. His story, however, was another matter. It was like a tale from the Twilight Zone.

Elizabeth set their empty plates in the sink and wiped crumbs off the table. "It was the least I could do after you got that piece of glass out of my heel and bandaged it." She looked at her foot, amused at the amount of gauze he had thought it necessary to use.

Her usual reticence and shyness seemed to have deserted her. Duncan had spun a fascinating, if unbelievable tale, and she was no longer in a hurry for him to leave. His story had captured her sympathy, and Angus was involved, spiking her curiosity. For the first time in a long time, she wanted something more than safety and solitude. She wanted to learn more about this compelling man, and her treasured ghost. "Would you like another cup of coffee, Mr. Munroe?"

"I'd love one. Please, call me Duncan."

"All right, Duncan." Elizabeth surreptitiously studied him while she filled his cup. His hands were large with short clean nails and a sprinkling of blonde hair on his knuckles. She always noticed a man's hands. His looked soft, yet strong. She would bet they would be warm.

Now where had that thought come from? "How long were you married?" she asked.

"Three years. My wife was twenty-nine when Angus Aberdeen murdered her."

She dismissed his ridiculous accusation, instead focusing on him. The frown line had deepened between his brows. So had the crinkles at the corners of his eyes. Laugh lines from another time in his life, she imagined. He looked like a thoughtful person with a sense of humor; like someone she would like to have known before his tragedy.

How would he react if she told him the killer he pursued was a dead man, a ghost who could not possibly have murdered an insect, yet alone a woman? With a few words, she could change his whole disposition. She could assure him of his mistake and free him to seek vengeance elsewhere.

She could, but she wouldn't. Duncan would no more believe her than she believed him. And, too, she would never betray Angus by admitting he lived here.

"She was so young," she murmured with compassion. "And you were married for such a short time." She touched his arm and let her fingers linger. "I'm so sorry for your loss. It must be very difficult for you."

"It is extremely difficult, Miss Barrett. The only thing that keeps me going is the desire to give her killer his just reward." His voice was deep and low. He spoke slowly, as if to suppress his pain.

"How long ago did this happen?"

"Four years. But, really, time has no meaning for me anymore."

Four years. The sharpness of new grief must surely have dulled by now, she thought. He should be well on his way to resuming a normal life--a life not driven by revenge.

She focused on his lips and tried to picture him smiling. His mouth turned down at the corners. It looked as if it would know how to kiss a woman just the right way. The perfect way.

She'd had all kinds of kisses from the men in her life. Hard, quick kisses from hard lips. Wet kisses from too-soft mouths. Distracted pecks that had left her feeling insignificant. Sweet kisses that had made her giggle. Duncan's mouth made her wonder about the kind of kiss she'd never known, but knew existed.

Heat scorched her face and torso. She must surely be glowing, she thought; burning from shame and exhilaration. She was treading wicked waters, yet she couldn't bring herself to turn away.

She played with her hair as her attention dropped from his face to the muscles that rippled beneath his shirt. To her shock, her mouth watered. She had a vivid mental impression of him tangling his fingers in her hair and kissing her senseless.

She almost gasped. What kind of magician was he to cast such a spell on her? She'd never had such inappropriate thoughts about someone she hardly knew. This wasn't at all like her.

She met his gaze, and then quickly averted her eyes. She'd been caught staring.

And now he was staring.

She must look frumpy and unappealing in her coffee-stained sweats and bedroom slippers. Why hadn't she put on jeans and a sweater?

His puzzled look turned into a smile when she snatched his still-full cup from the table. Not the smile she had imagined, but a smile nonetheless.

For a moment she had the impression he knew her thoughts. How embarrassing. Of course he couldn't read her mind, but it was apparent he found her amusing. Her chin shot up. For goodness sakes, he was a grieving widower. He was here to attempt to avenge his wife's death. He had other things on his mind, and she belonged to Angus.

Angus had apparently abandoned her for the time being. Considering her wayward musings, that was a good thing.

Chapter 7

Elizabeth washed dishes and cleaned the coffee pot while Duncan continued his tale of woe. She kept her back to him, relieved to find her awkward attraction had diminished. She slowed her chores, unwilling to turn around, but she hung on every word he said. The more he talked, the more uneasy she became.

"I find this very hard to believe," she said, snapping the dish towel and draping it over the oven handle. There was nothing to do but sit back down at the table with him. Even so, she was hesitant to make eye contact. She traced the red design on her old porcelain table with her finger. The metal was cold against her damp wrist. She shivered. "I've never heard of a ghost actually killing anyone. What makes you think he's come here, to my house?"

"Apparitions have been known to move from one place to another."

"Plattsburgh is a long ways away. I hardly think your ghost just up and flew over three hundred miles."

"I live in Plattsburgh now, but we lived closer to Midville when my wife was murdered."

"Why would he come to live in this house?"

Duncan took an envelope from his coat pocket. Inside, a few pieces of yellowed paper were folded. He slid them out and laid them on the table. "This is the original plat for this property, and the original deed of ownership. It shows this house was built by Angus Aberdeen in eighteen sixty-eight. He lived here until his death and then continued to stay here even after he died. He left this place long enough to kill my wife, and then he returned here."

Elizabeth bit her lip, averting her eyes from the deed. Anxious excitement flooded her. To unfold it and look at it would give him the impression she gave his ridiculous story credence. But, oh how she would love to get her hands on that piece of history. Perhaps it had Angus's actual signature. She wanted to see it. To run her finger over the ink that had flowed from the pen in her beloved's hand.

"How did she die?" As soon as the words were out of

her mouth she regretted them. She didn't really want to know, but Duncan was studying her as if he was waiting for a response.

"Angus stabbed her to death. It's vital that I find him before he kills again."

She felt like she'd been plunged into ice water. Suddenly it seemed very important Duncan never find out that Angus's spirit lived here with her. "I'm sorry, Duncan, but you must be wrong, I've never heard of Angus Aberdeen."

"Really?" One of his eyebrows rose enough to indicate he didn't believe her. "Have you never read the inscription on the tombstone?"

"What tombstone?"

"His bones are out there, but he is in here."

She was still trying to wrap her head around the idea of Angus being buried on her property when Duncan spoke again.

"I can tell you everything about Angus. Everything you want to know. And much more you should know for you own welfare."

Suddenly he seemed more intimidating than attractive. His blue eyes had deepened in color, turning somber and cold. She'd made a mistake. He had no business here, and she would be damned if she was going to continue to call him by his familiar name. "I don't think it's a good idea to go any further with this, Mr. Munroe. I've already told you this is the wrong place to look for the ghost of Angus Aberdeen."

Duncan ignored her. "He's Scottish, you know. He was an immigrant. He established his residence here in Midville for financial reasons."

"I don't need a history lesson." Her hands trembled. She folded them in her lap, unwilling for him to see how unsettled she was. *Where was the grave?* She'd been all over the property, burrowing deep into the blackberry bushes, digging out weeds from a long neglected flower garden. She'd spent weeks with new garden tools, manicuring the lawn when she'd first moved in.

"He was a cunning businessman with a talent for finances. He started one small business after another and hoarded his money. Eventually, he saved enough to buy up all the available mining rights in this county."

She put thoughts of the grave aside. For the past three years her imagination had conjured images and ideas about Angus. Of course she'd been curious. Of course she'd wondered if there was a way to find out who he had been and what his life had been like.

"Angus made his riches from coal, and then expanded into railroad stock." Duncan's tone was low and steady, almost mesmerizing. "His influence and reputation grew over the years. He became a man who was envied by most of his colleagues."

"Did he have a wife? Children?" She wasn't certain she wanted to know if Angus had been in love or had a family, although she was certain he must have.

"He never married."

How small of her to be relieved. If she truly cared about her ghost she would wish he had lived a life full of love and passion.

"In his late forties he became mayor of Midville," Duncan continued. "He served the town for six years and then he was elected to Congress. Women pursued him, but he had no interest in a romantic involvement and so remained unencumbered by a family."

Elizabeth wondered if she imagined the slight tone of bitterness that had crept into Duncan's voice.

"By the time Angus was fifty-four, he was one of the wealthiest men in the state. That was the year he built this house. He lived alone here for the rest of his life."

"How do you know so much about him? Are you related to him?"

An annoyed smile came and went so quickly she wasn't certain she'd seen it.

"You can research anyone and anything online," he said.

So you could. A thrill of apprehension stabbed her belly at the thought of Googling Angus. She knew she would never do that. It would, she told herself, take away the mystery. It would give too much of a dose of reality to her perfect fantasy world.

"So this pillar of the community lived here, continued to haunt the place after he died, and then left to kill your wife before high-tailing it back here?"

"The complete truth is a little more complicated, but yes, Elizabeth, that's what I am telling you."

She barely kept from snorting with derision. Duncan fascinated her. He knew things about Angus--things she wanted to learn. But his story was repelling and more than a little frightening. If he went on with it, he would insert his morbid fantasies into the facts. How could she have allowed him to fill her head with such nonsense?

"This is all very interesting Mr. Munroe," she said. "But, as I've already told you, I have never heard of Angus Aberdeen. Surely such a notable man would have a tangible legacy in Midville. A school named after him, or a street. I've been here three years. I've never heard of him."

"So it is back to Mr. Munroe, is it? I told you Angus was a wealthy, powerful man. I never said he was well-liked."

Elizabeth glanced at the clock and was shocked that it was well past noon. He had been here for four hours. She stood. Her chair skittered a few inches on the soapstone tiles. The sound set her teeth on edge. "Excuse me," she said, going to the cupboard and taking out a couple of cans of soup. She fussed at the counter, her back to him. Her hands fumbled with the can opener. "I'm expecting my brothers to come home any minute now. I'm afraid, as interesting as this conversation is, I have to start their lunch." *Please take the hint and leave.*

She wanted him gone. He'd come here uninvited and deliberately tried to change her perception of Angus. He had also made her feel inappropriate things that confused her and would certainly upset her beloved ghost.

"Angus was killed in this room on his sixty-fourth birthday," Duncan said. His voice was close. He'd come up behind her without making a sound.

Elizabeth whirled and knocked a cast iron frying pan off the stove. The clatter made them both jump. "I-I think you should go now, Mr. Munroe."

Duncan picked up the pan and set it on the counter. "Duncan." He took Elizabeth by the shoulders, turning her to face him. "You should listen to the rest of the story, Elizabeth. It involves you."

She shrugged Duncan's hands away. Her heart raced. "No! I don't want to hear anymore." She loved Angus. She didn't want to know the details of his death.

"Angus's closest friend was Andrew Grayson," he continued. "Andrew was a younger capitalist who arrived from the old country shortly after Angus. He was also Angus's biggest business rival. Andrew, too, built wealth in his adopted country. He eventually went back to Scotland for a short time and married a beautiful young woman. He brought her here to live in Midville. Her name was Elizabeth, too.

"Andrew's wife was an immoral siren. She enchanted Angus with a spell of lust and deceit he was powerless to break. As time went by his political life and his finances took a backseat to her charms. His friendship with Andrew deteriorated. His fascination with Elizabeth grew.

66

"He neglected his responsibilities and lost interest in his ventures. Eventually he lost his seat in congress and a good portion of his fortune, yet he could think of nothing but Elizabeth. He was obsessed with her. He grew to hate her, but couldn't live without their stolen moments.

"Andrew knew. One morning, he watched Elizabeth leave this house before dawn. She went directly to the cliffs and jumped to her death."

"Stop saying those horrible things," Elizabeth blurted. I don't believe you, so why waste your breath?"

"You will believe me before long. You will have no choice."

Elizabeth fell silent at the threat. How on earth was she going to get rid of him? She tried to appear impassive and uninterested as she looked past him, out the kitchen window. Her mind conjured an image of a young woman willingly jumping to her death from her back yard. Perhaps she was pushed. *No, it didn't happen.* She wasn't going to fall into Duncan's trap. He was lying. She briefly squeezed her eyes shut, trying to erase the mental image.

"Andrew found Angus here in the kitchen. It only took a single shot to claim his life."

"That can't be true! And it has nothing to do with me," Elizabeth cried, shaken.

"You are standing on his blood."

She looked down in disbelief. Duncan Munroe was insane. A nervous giggle surfaced before she could bite it back. "That stain is grease, Mr. Munroe. Someone dropped food there and the grease stained the tiles." And stained them well and forever it seemed. She had scrubbed the area with a passion several times to no avail. Each time she imagined a turkey or roast splattered on the floor, and the chagrin of the cook.

"It was a while before he was discovered," Duncan said. "His heart continued to pump until he bled out on that very spot. His life soaked into the floor and seeped through the cracks to the subflooring."

She wanted to block out Duncan's voice. She wished wholeheartedly she could undo the words that told her Angus's bones were in the yard, and his blood in the house. "What a ridiculous story. How could you possibly know any of that? And why would you tell me? I live in this house. Are you trying to scare me out of it?" She started shaking.

Duncan slid his arm over her shoulder. "I'm sorry, Elizabeth," he murmured against the top of her head. He stroked her back. "Believe me, I am not here to hurt or frighten you. I came to warn you. This is your home; there are things about it you have to know."

"No! I don't want to hear anymore. Just go. Please," she begged, her voice muffled against his shirt. Only minutes ago she had imagined him holding her. He felt as warm and strong as she had expected. His chest was hard, his muscles rolled beneath his shirt sleeves. She had no desire to linger in his embrace. He was a liar and perhaps, a raging lunatic. She stiffened and Duncan dropped his hands.

He picked up the deed slid it back into the envelope. "I'll leave for now, but I'm giving you Angus's diary. Promise me you'll read it."

Angus's diary? He had Angus's diary? How was that possible? And how had he obtained the original deed to this house? The diary and the deed were more lies. They were figments of Duncan's twisted imagination. She hadn't looked at the deed, but she was certain that it must a worthless piece of paper having nothing to do with Angus or this house. "Don't bother to leave the diary," she said. "I'm not going to read anything. My--our home is not haunted."

"You have no brothers, Elizabeth. There is no need to pretend. I know you are the only living inhabitant of this house. Nevertheless, you shouldn't be afraid of me. I came to help you."

"No, you didn't. In spite of what you say, you came here to deliberately frighten me. But you don't," she snapped. "And you know nothing about me, or how I live, or who I live with." She took a stance and angrily pointed to the front of the house. "Get out. I don't want to hear any more stupid stories about your ghost. I just want you to leave."

"He's your ghost, Elizabeth. And you are his." Duncan set a small, worn book on her table. "Read this. When you realize you need my help, call me on my cell phone." He slid the envelope with the deed into his pocket.

"Do you have something to write with, and a piece of paper?"

She opened the junk drawer to find a pen. Her birthday card was in there too. It had been ripped into several pieces. Her stomach twisted. Angus had gone into her purse.

She handed Duncan the pen and a portion of the card. Let him leave his number. It didn't matter as long as he left her alone. She didn't want it. She wouldn't use it, but the sooner he gave it to her, the sooner he would go away.

"This is my number. Put it somewhere safe," he said, scribbling on the torn piece of paper. "Better yet, memorize it. If for any reason you can't reach me on my cell phone, you can find me at the Lighthouse Inn." He slid the number towards her.

She looked away and tucked her arms beneath her arm pits.

"I know you will need me. I won't leave Midville until I hear from you. "It was a pleasure, my dear." He nodded politely and let himself out.

When she heard the front door slam, she dropped her arms and gave a sob of relief. Then she stood and stared at the diary.

Chapter **8**

Elizabeth's hands trembled as she jerked the swath of gauze from her foot and angrily balled it up. She was a fool. She should not have allowed Duncan Munroe to invade her home and her mind. He'd ruined her day off and filled her with suspicion. She had always imagined Angus to be a handsome young spirit, not a wicked old man. And she had come to consider her home to be a sanctuary, not a place that harbored evil.

Granted, she had not always felt this way. Chills made her shudder as she allowed her mind to take her back to a time best forgotten.

Her first impression of her inheritance had almost broken her resolve and sent her back to her home town. The overwhelming size and almost living countenance of the house had made her stomach twist. The weathered wood door was the color of mud and looked like a mouth forever frozen in a scream. The linings of the drawn drapes looked to be the shade of eyeballs; the windows had appeared to be staring blankly into something behind her. How could she possibly live in such a mausoleum?

Her aunt and uncle hadn't. For as far back as her memory took her, they had lived in a tiny Cape Cod house with green walls and steep steps to the bedrooms above and the basement below. She had only discovered the existence of the Mulberry Drive house and property at the reading of their will.

That first day, when she'd finally found the courage to approach the front door, she'd twisted the key with trembling fingers. The lock had clicked and the door had creaked open with no help from her.

Elizabeth caught herself staring at the ball of gauze in her hand. She went to the pantry and with little thought dropped it into a trash can. Her focus was still in the past, recalling an unpleasant experience she had not thought of in years.

She remembered that in those first moments after crossing the threshold, she'd had a fleeting but vivid impression of someone waiting for her. How had she found the courage to explore the house alone?

She remembered clutching her purse to her chest as she investigated each room.

The damp chill, even in the late summer afternoon, had made her teeth chatter. Echoes of her footsteps had followed her. Echoes that should not have happened because the house, though empty for some time, had been chocked full of furniture. Every few steps she had paused and glanced behind her. Each time something had seemed slightly out of place--something indefinably skewed from the last peek.

She had broached the living room with dread, maneuvering through a maze of mahogany tables and dark mohair sofas and chairs. The room was gloomy; the power had yet to be turned on. Thinking to let sunlight in, she had tugged at the heavy maroon velvet drapes. Like a noxious powder puff, the fabric had released a cloud of foul dust. Choking, she had backed away and rushed from the room.

The window overlooked the front entrance; there had been no lining on the drapes.

The somber parlor and the antiquated kitchen had appeared to be transported from another century. The amount of work needed to update the house would be overwhelming.

She had hurried away without going upstairs, anxious to be gone from the place before dark.

The next morning she had paid her hotel bill, taken her luggage and returned. Arriving at the house in the bright morning sunlight had made all the difference. The chill had dissipated. The rooms appeared cozy and welcoming.

She had carefully drawn back the drapes, firmly resolving to buck up and face the fact she had a new life ahead of her. It couldn't possibly be worse than the one she'd left behind. She had escaped a malignant relationship. She had left the suffocating solicitousness of her parents. There was nothing to be afraid of. Nothing at all.

She had quickly settled into her position at Clark's Insurance Agency. Her weekends and evenings had been spent scrubbing, vacuuming, polishing and waxing. The place had been neglected for a very long time. It didn't matter. It was hers now. Hers, complete with its history, charm and foibles.

She had worked to exhaustion, leaving little time to dwell on the things that never moved until she looked away.

It had taken no time at all for the presence of Angus to insinuate himself into her cognizance. He had come to her in small increments and charmed her with his ghostly antics. The unpleasant perception of things unseen must have been his way of introducing himself, and perhaps feeling her out. Indeed, the house had been his domain before she had intruded. Soon, the trepidation she'd felt upon arriving became a buried memory.

As she had come to know her ghost, she had come to hold him in great esteem. For the past several years, Angus had made this house the home of her heart. The tranquility and contentment he inspired in her had kept the desolation at bay—and the moving shadows still.

The whistling wind and a sharp gust of air startled Elizabeth out of her reverie. Duncan must have left the front door open. She shoved her slipper back on, grabbed a broom and dustpan and limped into the parlor. Her foot throbbed but she had to clean up the broken glass in the hallway.

With audible pops, flames appeared on every candle in the room. She gasped, clutching her hands to her heart. "Angus?" She dropped the broom. Had he been here all along, and heard everything Duncan had said? Surely, she would have been aware of his presence.

Something cold and moist brushed her neck. It stirred wisps of her hair and left a tingling trail across her scalp. She followed the sensations with her hands, trying to retain them. Wherever her fingers touched the lingering chill, they burned. She dropped her hands, balling them into fists. He knew. He'd been there, in the kitchen, eavesdropping. "I didn't believe him, Angus. Honest. And I didn't tell him about you. You know that."

The chandelier dimmed to black, the candles blew out, leaving the weak gloom of the winter afternoon as the only light. The temperature in the room became frigid. Elizabeth was familiar with Angus's temper tantrums. She knew what was coming. "No, Angus! Please don't leave."

The front door slammed with a crack that made her jump. Just like that, Angus was gone. Anguish coursed through her because the first touch he had ever given her had been in anger.

Would he come back? Would he forgive her for the momentary doubt she'd experienced? Her worst fear was that Angus knew about the desire she'd felt in the arms of a real man; the sharp need to have his very warm, very human touch linger on her skin.

Why had she felt those things? She would never have suspected she harbored such wanton behavior in her personality. She was disgusted with herself for being attracted to a man with deception on his mind.

What had Duncan really hoped to accomplish with his accusations? She would never know.

That night it took Elizabeth hours to calm her raging thoughts enough to fall asleep. When she did, she dreamed of two men.

When she awoke in the morning she felt satiated and languorous. She hadn't spent the night alone. Angus had returned and finally joined her in her bed.

She smiled and stretched. So ghosts were as jealous as mere mortal men. The thought might have been amusing if she were not slightly apprehensive of both Duncan and his insane accusations, and Angus. Not that there could be any physical retribution from her ghostly paramour if he did suspect her emotional indiscretion. No, Angus would never hurt her that way.

Still, she had no doubt he could make her wretched if

he chose.

Elizabeth arrived at work a half hour earlier than usual. She'd brought a broom with her, much to the amusement of the taxi driver. Snow had fallen steadily for forty-eight hours. As expected, her car looked like a giant marshmallow, its form distorted by a thick covering of snow.

She poked and prodded the crusty covering with the broom handle and then swept the broken chunks off her aging Taurus. Another New England winter like this and she might have to buy a car with four-wheel drive.

There was another snow-covered car nearby. Someone else had apparently left their vehicle in the company parking lot overnight. She leaned her broom against it and went inside the building.

Cold and huffing from exertion she went into the break room for a cup of coffee and bumped into Christy.

Christy brushed by her, leaving the beverage station without a word.

Elizabeth made her coffee hot and sweet and rolled the cup in her hands until she could feel her fingers again. She hung up her coat and changed into the Sherpa boots she had left beneath her desk Monday afternoon. It was seven minutes to nine but the phones were already buzzing.

Elizabeth approached Christy. "Is something wrong?"

"I had as much to drink as both of you. I didn't call in

with a hangover."

"Neither did I," Elizabeth said, stung. "I didn't feel well but I wasn't hung over."

"Jody and I were the only ones here yesterday and she left at noon for a doctor's appointment. I can't do the work of four people."

"I'm sorry. Perhaps I should have come in, ill or not. Where was Angela?"

"I have no idea. I only know she wasn't here."

"I had something important to do," Angela said, shrugging out of her coat. She stomped her feet and brushed snow from her hair and her pant legs. "So I took a personal day." She hung her coat on the rack and turned to Christy. "So what?"

"You could have warned me at Damon's. You never said a word."

"I didn't know at the time, and who would have thought you'd call in, too, Liz. You never take time off."

"I was sick," Elizabeth protested.

"You took off and left me there," Christy said, obviously upset. "Why would you do that?"

Elizabeth stiffened and folded her arms beneath her breasts. "You know I wasn't feeling well."

"Not you, Liz. Her." Christy jerked her chin at Angela. "You just took off and left me at Damon's. I waited for you until the driver threatened to leave without me. I felt ridiculous, alone in that limo."

"I told you I was going."

"You said you'd be back."

"Lower your voice, Christy," Angela said mildly. "Something came up. I'm really sorry."

"It must have been important to blow me off like that."

"It was. Can we leave it at that, please?"

Mr. Clark approached them. "Angela," he said without preamble. "I would appreciate a little more notice next time you need a personal day." He nodded briefly at Christy and Elizabeth and left before Angela could respond. For a moment the only sound was his footsteps on the parquet floor

Angela threw up her arms. "Geez, I'm sorry."

"And that makes everything okay?" Christy asked. Her voice had risen so high it nearly squeaked. It was apparent she was not in a forgiving mood. "Next time we go out together, we leave together."

The day was off to an uncomfortable start, Elizabeth thought, wishing she had taken a second day off.

Christy's mouth was an angry red slash. She turned away, her head and shoulders rigid as she walked down the hall.

Angela had purple smudges beneath her bloodshot eyes and looked slightly ill. Mr. Clark had reprimanded her in front of them, something he had never before done.

Elizabeth shriveled inside. She hated confrontation. This was all the results of her birthday party. There would be no celebrating next year if she had anything to say about it.

Angela shrugged and gave a half smile to Elizabeth. "Since your car was all cleaned off, I assume you're the one who left the broom for me. Thanks. I left it by your car."

So, Elizabeth thought, primly, Angela obviously hadn't gone home from Damon's. She still wore the same red mohair sweater and slim black skirt she'd worn Monday. If her self-satisfied expression was an indication, she had probably been up to something Elizabeth would never do.

As soon as the distasteful thought blossomed, she tamped it down. She had no right to judge Angela or anyone. She'd spent her day off attempting to seduce a frightening stranger and then arguing with a ghost before making up with him and spending a delicious night in his ephemeral embrace.

If Christy and Angela ever found out about her private life she would lose their friendship. They would, most likely, think she was insane. Perhaps she was.

Chapter 9

Sunday morning promised to be yet another miserable day. Winter raged outside of Elizabeth's home, icing over bushes and trees. Ferocious wind gusts sent salt spray up the cliff. The seas below roared and thrashed.

She peered through the window and shivered. She always went to Sunday service and then stopped for groceries on the way home. What harm would it do to skip church for once? She shrugged away a faint miasma of guilt and decided to stay home. She could stay in her nightgown and get lost in a good book.

She made a cup of tea in the microwave, noticing

Duncan's cell phone number was still on the counter. She thought she had thrown it away. She crumpled the piece of paper and stuffed it into the junk drawer.

She took her tea into the living room, wrapped an old quilt around her legs and reached for her half-read novel. Her hand fell instead on the diary. She hadn't touched it since Duncan left, except to put it in a cupboard, out of sight. And now it was here. "You want me to read this, Angus?"

The book shifted beneath her palm.

"But--why?" Heart slamming, she opened the cracked, yellowed pages. The penmanship was precise. The ink had faded to shades of brown that almost looked like old blood. "I don't believe this is yours." She ran her fingers over the handwriting.

I cannot think of anything but her. I have no desire to focus on my career, my aspirations or my businesses. I do not think she is aware of the spell she has woven around me. She pretends to regret our affair, but I know better. I know she cannot break from me any more than I can leave her. I think Andrew must know. I think she may have told him to salve her conscience, or perhaps to destroy the bond between Andrew and me. I wish she'd never been born. She will be the death of me. If only I had the will to strangle her before she destroys me. But I am a weak man, unwilling to part with her just yet.

Elizabeth tossed the fragile missive aside like it was

on fire. She was right. The weak, obsessed person who wrote those words couldn't possibly be her Angus. He knew if she read the diary it would vindicate him. She would know for certain Duncan lied.

She remembered how she slowly became aware of Angus.

Broken when she came to Midville, she had wanted nothing from life but a quiet place for her spirit to heal. She had felt insignificant and unworthy and certain she was destined to remain alone.

But Angus was here, waiting for her.

He hadn't frightened or threatened her, even when he wrote his name in old-fashioned script on her steamy bathroom mirror.

After her initial shock, she came to laugh at his ways of announcing his presence. He opened and then slammed cupboard doors. He rang bells in distant rooms in her fusty old mansion and lighted candles to greet her after work.

He seemed to know her, and bestowed upon her lovely scents. They were of things remembered, like cream soda, which always took her back to her fifth birthday party, cut grass, sunscreen and Lily of the Valley perfume-- the smell of her mother.

Her most favorite gift from him was an elusive candy flavor that burst in her mouth at unexpected moments. It must have been imprinted on her mind when she was too young to understand what it represented, but the vague idea of carnival music came with it.

It took no time at all for her to become infatuated with him. She was delighted and soothed by the presence of a benevolent, romantic male being.

She had blossomed in their private world because Angus made her feel cherished.

Elizabeth glared at the diary. It had fallen on the floor and was open to the page she had read. The handwriting was similar to Angus's mirror signature, but this wasn't his diary. Her ghostly cohabiter could never have contemplated murder.

As if to reward her for her loyalty, Angus made himself known. A fire burst into flame in the fireplace. The chilly room warmed and she threw off the quilt, anticipation blossoming in her heart.

A moist brush against her neck, hot and thrilling, sent sparks down her spine. Her breath caught in her throat. All her pent up passion finally surfaced. With a soft cry, she opened like a flower enticing a hummingbird. Arms wide, head lolling back against her chair, she closed her eyes and waited.

Angus didn't disappoint her. Wave after wave of effervescence washed over her, through her. Her skin peaked and swelled with arousal. Her mind echoed with a rumbling voice, murmured words she couldn't quite make out. Yearning such as she'd never experienced stole her breath. The fire crackled, the room spun. She moaned as she began a slow slide into a delirium of pleasure.

"Oh, Angus! Oh!" Her own voice brought her back to

reality. Sitting up, she straightened her nightgown. She felt the heat of her blush as she wiped tears from her cheeks.

And then she laughed. Old man, indeed. Her Angus was youthful and virile. But she couldn't help thinking that he was also very, very dead.

After Angus's lovemaking, Elizabeth felt energized. The wind had died down so she decided to get some fresh air. She got out of her nightgown, bundled up and walked around her property until she couldn't feel her hands and her feet began to ache in her Sherpa boots.

She spent most of the time thinking about Angus. Her love for him was growing with each passing hour. She wished she had known him when he was alive. Had he really built this home? Where did he go when he left her alone? She would have been aware of him had he stayed in the house.

She was never aware of him when she was outside.

She searched everywhere for his tombstone, even peering into the depths of the denuded briar patch that formed an impenetrable barrier in summer. She found nothing. The relief was immense. It made it easy to dismiss everything else Duncan had told her.

Twilight finally turned the snow-covered lawn on the west side of the stone house pink, and conjured cold blue shadows on the east side by the cliffs. She stood at the cliff edge, hugging herself, watching gulls circle and dive until they disappeared in the darkening distance. Where, she wondered, did seagulls spend the night?

Her teeth started to chatter. Tremors shook her chest. She needed to get warm but didn't want to go inside and face the diary. Unfortunately, tomorrow was Monday and she had laundry to do.

Gathering up a basket of dark slacks and knit tops, Elizabeth forced herself to open the small door inside the pantry that led to steep, narrow cellar steps. The door was made of tongue and groove planks and sat crooked on its hinges. It closed tight at the bottom, but the top cocked away from the frame, allowing fetid air to escape into the house. She'd added a slide lock to hold it shut, but the warped wood had pulled the screws loose.

She took a deep breath and tugged the string that followed the low overhead through a series of screw-hooks and was attached to the single light bulb that hung at the foot of the steps. The passage was barely wide enough to squeeze through with the plastic basket.

As usual, when she came down here the fine hair on her arms and the back of her neck rose in an unpleasant tickle. She quickly stuffed the clothes into the washer and started it. She set the empty basket on the dryer, wondering once more, how such large appliances had been maneuvered down that narrow passage. Her parent's house had two steel doors that opened to their basement. What would she do if the dryer couldn't be repaired and had to be replaced?

She snatched the sheets from the old clothesline that hung between the overhead beams. She rolled them into balls and stuffed them into the basket. She would take them to the balcony and shake them well, just in case there were any spiders on them.

The light bulb swung slightly from its cord, making shadows jerk and briefly illuminating dark, unused corners. She'd never explored the basement before. Perhaps there was an exterior door that had been boarded off although she had never seen one in her foundation.

Staring through the gloom, she barely picked out narrow, dirt encrusted glass windows that surely must be behind the boxwood hedge. Maybe the door was there, beneath or next to the windows. If she could find it, she could open it and let some light in. Wishing she had a flashlight, she took a couple of steps towards the windows.

She walked into a spider web. It stuck to her face and hair. Shuddering, trying not to scream, she closed her eyes and clawed at the sticky strands. When she opened them she was facing a different direction. The cellar in front of her disappeared far into the darkness under the kitchen. It was an area from which she always averted her eyes, imagining rats and snakes and things that would attack and bite her.

She turned away, rolling the web on her fingers. She couldn't shake it loose so she wiped it onto her pants. When she looked up she was standing beneath the kitchen floor. Her heart thrummed. Her throat tightened, as did every muscle in her body. She hadn't moved, had she?

Cold swirled around her. The washer clicked from filling to agitating, the sounds coming at her from all directions. She was disoriented and dizzy. "Angus," she cried, weakly. "I need you." Trying to focus on the light bulb, she took another step and froze.

She had to look.

It took a few moments for her vision to adjust to the weak dregs of light that illuminated the old plank subflooring over her head. She could make out very few details, except for one. The stain. It spread in an obsidian irregular pattern against the lighter shades of dark. It was the same pattern as the grease stain on the soapstone tiles.

Her vision became more acute. The weak illumination was enough to show she stood in the middle of the same pattern on the dirt floor.

With a cry, she ran towards the light bulb and then stumbled up the steps. She burst through the door, into her pantry, gasping from holding her breath.

Then she giggled.

She'd spooked herself. She had let her imagination take reign and scared the daylights right out of herself. How foolish. Her mind dismissed the stain as a product of her imagination. It didn't exist. But that spider web had been real, and huge. It was probably made by a huge spider.

The clothes basket was still in the cellar. Too bad. She wasn't going to go back down there.

In fact, the clothes she'd washed were items she seldom wore. They could stay right where they were until she had an electrician inspect the dryer. She would have him install more light down there. A lot more light. Then she would go down to get her clothes--while he was down there.

She plucked the web from her pants and wiped it onto a crumpled paper towel in the trash can. She needed a bath and a good shampoo.

She tried to ignore the diary but after passing it a dozen times, she found herself wanting to read more. It wasn't Angus's diary, but someone had written it. She felt compelled to find out more about that long ago person with the murderous intent.

She put on old flannel pajamas, took the diary and climbed into the four-poster bed that perhaps Angus had slept on. She didn't know the history of any of the beautiful pieces of furniture that were now hers, but assumed they dated back to the original owner. Had Angus chosen them?

It was only eight-thirty but felt more like midnight. She turned on her reading lamp and opened the diary to a random page.

As I plan her demise, I find I've begun to enjoy my own imagination more than the moments I spend with her. I want to plunge a knife into her heart. I can feel her warm blood on my hands. I want to run them across my face. I would give half my fortune to taste her blood on my fingers. But the time has not yet come. She will be allowed to bear the child she told me she is to have. I am a patient man.

Tossing the diary aside, Elizabeth bolted out of bed. She had to talk to Angus. She needed to be reassured that the man who penned these thoughts was not the ghost she loved.

"Angus!" She waited for the shift in the air, the certain knowledge in her heart that told her he was with her. He remained elusive. She went into every room in the house, calling for him. There was nothing to indicate he heard her.

He must have known she needed him in the cellar. Why hadn't he come to her then? He must know she wanted him now. Where was he?

Hours passed. If Angus heard her pleas he ignored them. Was he angry because she'd spent time alone, outside? Or did he feel guilty over past sins? That thought made her feel guilty and disloyal.

Would he ever return? She couldn't stand to think he might leave her forever.

She paced and pleaded to no avail. This was all Duncan's fault. It had been five days since his visit. Five days since he'd stormed into her life and gifted her with the damned diary. Duncan said he would remain in Midville until he heard from her. She came to the conclusion Angus would stay away until she convinced

Duncan to return to Plattsburgh. That meant she would have to call his cell phone. Thank goodness she hadn't thrown away the number.

She would invite him over and return the diary without letting him know she had read any of it.

The thought of Duncan returning to her home set off a wave of anxiety. It had to be done, but she felt herself falling back into her old habits of self-doubt and insecurity. She had made a perfect fool of herself in front of him. She'd been inappropriately flirty and argumentative. Suspecting he was mentally distraught, she'd nevertheless egged him on in an attempt to appease her curiosity. She'd lied and accused him of lying, and kicked him out of her house. Her behavior had been inexcusable.

The man would have to be insane to want to return at her invitation.

Chapter **10**

Elizabeth had invited Duncan for supper and it was almost done. Chowder simmered on the stove. The kitchen was redolent with the yeasty aroma of baking rolls.

All day at work she had rehearsed in her mind the words she would use to tell him to go away. Some perverse notion of hospitality, and anxiety at the thought of enforcing her will made her decide to approach him after they ate.

"Would you like something to drink while the rolls bake?" she asked.

Duncan sat, relaxed in her overstuffed chair in the parlor. "No, thanks, I'm fine. Can you sit for a minute?" he asked.

"For a moment, perhaps," she said, sitting on the sofa across from him.

"Have you ever felt the presence of evil here, Elizabeth?"

"Never," she insisted, pushing away the little things that were none of his business.

"Has anything unusual taken place in this house since you moved in?"

"Of course not." She refused to meet Duncan's intense gaze, concentrating instead on the photos he'd placed on her coffee table. They were of a laughing woman--a woman who resembled her in some ways, with long chestnut hair and a full, expressive mouth. "Your wife was beautiful, Duncan. You must miss her very much."

"I do." He tossed one more picture atop the others.

Elizabeth bit back a scream when she saw the pooling blood and wide, sightless eyes staring back at her. "How dare you?" She pushed the photos toward him. "Put them away!"

He left the pile on the table. "Does the blood frighten you? Is it too horrible to imagine her life ending like that?"

"That was unnecessary." She kept her eyes averted. "Why would you carry such a terrible reminder of her death around with you?"

He set more pictures down and fanned them out.

She didn't want to look but she couldn't stop from glancing at them. They were gory images of the dead woman. "Why would you keep those pictures? That's sick."

"I'm trying to convince you Angus is evil and dangerous," Duncan said.

She shot to her feet. "A ghost couldn't do that! You're insane if you think your imaginary killer ghost has anything to do with me or my home. Take your horrible pictures and get out of here!"

Duncan stood and took her arm. "Steady now. I mean you no harm. I assure you, I am as sane as you, Elizabeth. Don't send me away. I've only known you a short time, but I feel a connection between us."

They both looked at his grip on her arm. He relaxed his fingers but didn't remove his hand.

"You feel it, too," he said.

She jerked away. "Then why are you fixated on the past? You have a future, Duncan. But you have to let go of the pain. Forget your idea of a ghost murdering your wife. Destroy those photos." She lightly touched his shoulder and lowered her voice to a soothing tone. "Go home."

"Not yet. I've suffered a great loss. You give me comfort. You make me feel like my life isn't over. You make me believe in the future."

"I'm not going to accept that kind of oppressive responsibility, Duncan. I'm not the answer to your grief. I won't be. Go home. Leave me in peace."

"I can't just walk away from you." He plowed his fingers through his hair in a gesture that was almost desperate. "I need you. And, believe it or not, you need me."

Pity for him overrode everything else. The man was a basket case, she thought, tearing up. He apparently had no control over his desolation, and therefore wasn't responsible for his ridiculous behavior. If only she could make him forget about Angus and Beth. If only she could erase those horrible pictures from his mind--and hers.

Duncan tentatively hugged her. Her emotions were in an upheaval. She tightened her muscles but then she relaxed against him. He was right about one thing. He needed her. Feeling necessary was a heady experience. She had always been the needy one. Her arms snaked around his neck. Wanting to soothe and comfort them both, she pressed her lips to his.

Duncan returned her kiss, running his warm, moist mouth over her eyelids, cheeks and jaw.

Moaning softly, she sagged against him, reveling in the intimate touch. She opened her mouth beneath his and forgot the horror in which they were embroiled. It had been a very long time since she'd been caressed by a flesh and blood man.

A part of her mind watched her, judged her. This was wrong. She was betraying Angus. She was taking advantage of a grieving, unstable man.

At the moment she didn't care, she simply wanted more.

He stroked her back and returned her caresses, but

refrained from the intimacy she craved.

She willed him to know he had permission to do anything he chose. She pressed closer. Once more she found his mouth with hers.

He responded for a moment and then broke the kiss and rested his chin on her head. His body stiffened enough to let her know he had withdrawn emotionally. His arms loosened, finally dropping to his side, but he didn't withdraw.

She waited for her heart to settle and the heat to leave her face. Finally she stepped back and turned away, unable to face him. She'd misread his concern for attraction and was aghast that she had somehow allowed Duncan to turn the tables on her.

What kind of woman was she? She loved Angus. Angus was the source of her desire. He alone had awakened her in ways she never thought possible. Why was she so irresistibly drawn to a man who threatened to disturb the comfortable life she shared with Angus. "What would you do if you thought you'd found the ghost of Angus Aberdeen?" she asked when she felt composed enough to turn to him.

"Father Cornelius from St. Patrick's is ready to perform a ritual to persuade him to leave his earthy haunts forever."

"Exorcism?" She cringed inside. "Are you mad? I won't allow such nonsense in my home."

All the pity she had felt for him was evident in his

eyes. Pity for her. "Get out."

It was obvious he wanted to say more. Instead, he shrugged into his coat and left without another word.

Smoke rolled from the kitchen. "The rolls!" she cried. They were burned to small charred lumps. She flung them into the snow and set the pot of chowder outside her kitchen door on the porch beneath the balcony where the cold would keep it fresh. Her appetite was gone. Supper was a waste, and a precious opportunity had been lost. She certainly hadn't tried hard enough to convince Duncan to leave Midville.

Only then did she realize he'd left the photographs.

Elizabeth averted her eyes from the pictures on her coffee table and went to draw the heavy brocade drapes. Instead, she paused and stared through the glass into the night. What was happening to her perfect life? The comfort of her home had been invaded. She wanted to erase all memory of Duncan. To brush away the turmoil he'd left behind. If only he'd taken those damned pictures. She would burn them. She would. Her muscles tensed with the need to destroy them before she went to bed.

The reflection of a man in the glass caught her attention. Whirling, she found herself alone in an empty room. She looked back at the window. The reflection was gone. Had the vision been her imagination or had she caught a brief glimpse of Angus?

Suddenly the overpowering scent of roses filled the room. "Angus?" she whispered. "Were you here all along?

You were. You were spying on us."

Guilt twisted in her chest as she tried to recall her words and actions. Had she said anything disloyal? The caresses she'd shared with Duncan could be explained away as sympathy if Angus hadn't eavesdropped on her mind.

An old fear made her stomach clench. Common sense told her this was no mortal man with heavy fists. Angus wouldn't, couldn't beat her down in a rage. Still . . .

"You were thinking of me."

Startled, she jerked. "Oh!" Her hands crossed over her racing heart. This was the first time he had communicated with spoken words. "No," she said. "I wasn't thinking about you."

"You were."

She was thrilled at the sound of his voice. But why had he kept his presence unknown to her? What kind of game was he playing?

Or was he afraid of Duncan for some reason? The thought was ridiculous. No ghost would be afraid of a human.

"Admit it, Elizabeth."

"I thought about you in the cellar." Her first vocal exchange with her beloved and she couldn't keep the accusatory tone from her voice. "I needed you down there, Angus. And I needed you after I read that damned diary. Where were you?"

"I was with you."

"Yet you chose to let me believe I was alone with my fear and doubts."

"You should have more faith in me." His voice came from a different direction. "While he was spinning his lies and playing on your sympathy, I was in your thoughts."

Angus had remained aloof in her need. Now he demanded her attention, but this was the wrong time for him to confront her. She was too raw and confused from Duncan's accusations.

She had to think. She had to get away from him. The only way she knew how was to leave the house. Angus never accompanied her in the gardens. But it was dark and cold out there. She'd always been afraid of the dark.

The balcony. She would go there; it was outside the house.

"You can't avoid me."

She ran up the stairs, grabbing her coat from the hall tree as she passed. She slammed her bedroom door behind her. A hysterical laugh bubbled in her throat at the foolish gesture. She shrugged into her coat, but she never made it to the double doors.

A light touch gathered her hair at her nape. A jolt of heat seared the side of her neck and then traveled in excruciatingly slow degrees to every part of her body. The intimate touch disoriented her, flooding her with pleasure and anticipation. Her breath hitched in her throat, leaving her dizzy and gasping.

"Yes. Yes, I was thinking of you." Her anger

dissolved into sparks of greed and suffocating want. All thoughts of escaping from Angus flew right out of her head. "Is that what you want to hear? I'm always thinking of you."

His low laugh filled the room with the unmistakable sound of triumph.

Her coat flew from her, landing in the shadows of a far corner. She gulped when her dress slid down her body, becoming a puddle of soft fabric at her feet.

The dry heat of his foreplay turned into a bath of moist breath. Spears of desire shot through her. She was pulled, helplessly, into a vortex of flash and fire and bone deep joy. This was her Angus. This was her lover. Her safe lover, with whom she instinctively knew she could abandon herself. He would take her to the wicked and wonderful places in her heart and soul with no repercussions.

"You're mine."

Did she hear those words or imagine them?

"Forever."

Forever. It was what she had always wanted, to belong to someone forever. Someone who would love her and receive all the pent up love she had to give.

The need to touch him was overwhelming. Desperately seeking the weight and warmth of him, she reached for the elusive source of pleasure. Her rocking, nudging body made no contact. She closed her eyes, attempting to grasp with her imagination what she couldn't with her arms. Try as she might, the features she'd seen in the reflection wouldn't come back to her. Angus was her destiny, yet there was no warmth, no weight and no substance.

"Say it."

She raised her arms behind her head, running her fingers through her hair, letting it drift back to her shoulders. She slid her hands to her peaking breasts. Her own touch was too delicate. She tried to conjure the feeling of hard, rough hands and strong caresses. Instead, her womb vibrated like the plucked strings of a harp. The pleasure became torture, as if she were bound and unable to protest or participate in the erotic assault. She sobbed with the desire to reciprocate.

"Say it."

Her need for him grew until it was almost beyond bearing. Yet deep in the far recesses of her mind Duncan's voice nagged her. *"Have you ever felt the presence of evil here, Elizabeth?"*

"Never!" She doubled over, shoving her fists to her ears, and screamed, "Get out of my mind!"

"Say it!" Angus roared. The words came from beyond her walls with the blasting, frigid fury of a storm, thrusting her balcony doors open as if to warn her she could not have escaped him out there.

"Please, Angus, please . . ." She no longer knew for what she pleaded. But she knew what he wanted, what he demanded, and she wasn't going to give it to him. She couldn't have all of him. She refused to relinquish all of herself.

His aura flashed hot then cold, making her skin contract with electric spasms that skittered across her flesh. She trembled with need. It battered her helpless body like churning waves sucking her beneath the sea, tumbling her until she no longer knew up from down. Evil from innocence. Lies from truth.

He battered, pummeled and punished her with emotional and physical sensations that made her want to leap out of her own skin. Pain and pleasure beyond anything she could have imagined. She'd abhorred the physical abuse she had suffered from mortal men. Yet this maelstrom seemed created to her specific, deep, dark desires. Oh, Angus knew her well.

"Yes. I'm yours," she finally cried. Unable to resist him anymore, she sank to the floor and gave herself up to him.

Chapter 11

Duncan showed up after work Tuesday evening. Rain dripped off his hat. His overcoat was sodden. Angry black clouds swirled in the sky behind him. He carried a bottle of wine and a huge bouquet of lilies. "Please forgive me, Elizabeth. I never meant to hurt you." He gave her a sheepish grin. "I came to apologize. May I come in? I won't stay long."

She wasn't happy to see him and wanted to tell him to leave, but she couldn't bring herself to be rude. His misery over his wife's death must have been behind his aberrant behavior. Surely time would help him see how impossible his accusations were.

"Don't you believe in umbrellas?" she asked.

"I only have two hands and these were more important." He thrust the bouquet at her like a child offering wildflowers to his mother.

She took the flowers, peering around the overpoweringly fragrant blossoms. They were wet and cold and she wanted nothing more than to get them out of her hands.

Duncan's expression was guileless and expectant. She could tell he wanted something. To her shock, compassion blossomed in her heart again. It seemed to be a response to him she couldn't control. Yes, she wished he'd never come into her life. But pity for this gentle man made her want to console him before she sent him on his way. In truth, she owed him because she was certain Angus's ardor would never have surfaced without the catalyst of jealousy.

"Thank you," she said. "They're beautiful." They were more appropriate for a funeral, perhaps, but thoughtful, nevertheless. "You may as well come in and stay for supper." She was certain she didn't have to warn him to avoid talking about Angus. She was determined to make him take the diary and photographs when he left, but she wouldn't bring them up until the evening was over.

While she put the lilies in a vase and reheated the chowder, he brought in split logs from the back porch and started a fire.

He poured the wine he'd brought into her fragile crystal goblets. Then he rummaged through her CDs and put several bluesy instrumentals on to play.

The music awoke something in her that had been dormant: the joy of worldly entertainment. This was contemporary music, quite different than that conjured by Angus. His offerings were always well chosen, flooding her with tranquility from within, but this music plucked at her from outside her body. She bobbed her head and swayed her shoulders like she had in Damon's. She tapped her feet. Her smile felt strange and unused.

She realized she had become too withdrawn. She couldn't remember the last time she had seen a movie or eaten at a restaurant. She almost laughed at a sudden vision of herself as an old reclusive lady. No wonder Christy and Angela were gradually drifting away. She made a vow to try to reengage with the world around her.

Elizabeth sat next to Duncan on the floor in front of the crackling fire. They ate chowder and sipped wine while the hours melted into an intoxicating interlude. Thunder rumbled and the surf crashed in time to the music as they talked about everything except Angus and Duncan's wife.

Duncan set his bowl aside and stood. He increased the volume on her CD player and then took her hand and tugged her to her feet.

Lulled by the music, she snuggled into him, hiding her smile against his shirt as they danced to the plaintive wail of a saxophone.

"Beth."

"Hmmm?"

"Her name was Beth."

Elizabeth shivered. He was talking about his wife again.

"Does anyone ever call you Beth?" he asked, leaning back to rub his thumb across her lower lip.

"No!" She angrily jerked away. The mellow mood had been broken. "You didn't come to apologize. You came to convince me a ghost killed your wife."

"I came to tell you about Beth and about all the women

Angus murdered."

"Oh, Duncan, stop. I don't want to hear this!" Her stomach clenched. Once again she had totally misread a man's character.

"They were all named after the first Elizabeth."

She wanted to slap him. It was the first time in her life she had ever wanted to strike someone, but he was too persistent. He was never going to convince her Angus was a serial killer.

"Andrew had a daughter," he said. "She was named Elizabeth after her mother. She was an intelligent child who grew up to become a professor of history at New Haven University--an unheard of position for a woman in those days. Andrew was proud of her, yet filled with unease. He felt rebuked by God for his refusal to make the conscious choice to forgive. *'Do not condemn so that you will not be condemned.'*

"Andrew's wife had a child?" Elizabeth gasped. "How could she take her own life and leave a baby behind?" Everything Duncan said shocked her more than the last.

"Aye, she did. You will understand soon enough. Andrew's daughter married the owner of a mill. When they started their family his joy finally assuaged his terrible grief. When Elizabeth's first child, a girl, was born he forgave his wife, and he forgave Angus. He even chose to pray for their souls.

"Andrew's peace of mind infuriated Angus. His daughter's happiness was a thorn in Angus's side, so he killed her as though he had the right."

"Angus was dead!" she cried. "You want me to believe Angus killed Andrew's daughter even though he was long dead before she grew up?"

"Angus died a human death, but his essence never died. It is all around us. I feel it at this very moment. I smell it."

"You're mad," she managed.

"Mad, am I? Then why don't you call the police?" He reached out and gently grasped a lock of her hair, massaging the strands between his fingers. "Or, simply order me to leave?"

She recoiled. Why didn't she do either? There was something about watching him become unglued that was akin to watching a train wreck. She couldn't turn away. She couldn't block out the horror. She could only anticipate that whatever more came out of his mouth was certain to be fantastical. She braced herself to reject every word.

"Thirty years later, to the day of her death," Duncan continued, "Angus murdered Andrew's granddaughter, Elizabeth Grayson Cleary. She, too, was a young wife and mother."

"You're wasting your history lesson on me, Duncan. I can't keep track of all of those women. I'm not interested, anyway."

Sometime during his soliloquy, the music that had made her so happy stopped. As soon as Duncan left she was going to destroy those CDs. He'd ruined a special evening and made her feel like she had fallen into a horrific version of Alice's rabbit hole. She would never be able to listen to them without conjuring the alarm and revulsion she now felt.

It suddenly occurred to her this was what he wanted. It was what he'd planned from the beginning. He meant to frighten her. Why? What did he have to gain? "I want you to leave now."

"Elizabeth Grayson Cleary had two children, a son and a daughter—Andrew's great-grandchildren," he persisted.

"I'm sure your ghost killed her, too. I don't care!" She fought to keep from screaming at him. "I don't want to hear another word. Now I am ordering you to leave."

"There is no need to raise your voice. Yes, Angus killed

that poor, innocent creature and left her two children motherless. He killed her like he killed my Beth." His mouth hardened. So did his tone. "He used the same knife."

"Knife? Listen to yourself, Duncan, You aren't making sense. Even if, as you claim, Angus's spirit remained, he was simply that, a nebulous element with no ability to manipulate physical objects." She knew better, but she would never admit it.

"How do you know about these women?" She fought to keep the disdain from her voice. "This crazy story isn't something you discovered on the Internet. You're making it up. You should stop chasing ghosts and go home, Duncan. Seek help." She might as well have spoken to the walls.

"Andrew's great-granddaughter's name was also Elizabeth," Duncan persisted. "Everyone called her Livy. He hardened his heart against her, knowing if he allowed himself to love her it would instigate Angus's wrath. And that was the death of Andrew.

"Livy had two daughters, Betty and Susan. Andrew was gone, but Angus remained. That monster murdered Livy and Betty on the same day."

Elizabeth clamped her hands over her ears. "Enough. My head is spinning." If he wouldn't leave, she would have to. She darted a glance at the hallway.

"You will stay right here if you know what's good for you."

The soft-spoken threat made her shiver.

"Susan had twin girls," Duncan said. "But she named neither of them Elizabeth. Her grandchildren were not so lucky. Susan was my own Beth's grandmother. Angus Aberdeen murders every woman descendent who carries the name of Andrew's unfaithful wife."

Elizabeth shivered. Her grandmother's name was Susan. Her mother and her aunt Marguerite were twins. She would not ask the names of Susan's daughters. She didn't want to know. If he knew the names of her mother and aunt, it would prove Duncan had done research on her. That would make him a psychopath.

Chapter **12**

Elizabeth had bounced from disbelief to absolute fear to disdain and now fear again. The chaotic emotions made her nauseous. She'd been a fool to let Duncan in the door this evening. A man as disturbed as he was could certainly be dangerous.

She desperately wanted him to go away. Her cell phone was in her purse, hanging on the hall tree. If she tried to use it there was no telling what he would do. She had to keep him talking while she figured out how to get rid of him before he did her harm. "How did Andrew's daughter die?"

"She was bludgeoned to death, like her grandmother."

"Her grand--grandmother?" she stuttered. This last piece of information was simply too much to comprehend. She clapped her hand to her forehead and then dragged it slowly over her poor aching head. "You are not making any sense."

"Andrew's wife was the second Elizabeth Angus murdered. The first Elizabeth he killed was her mother."

She gasped. "Andrew's wife wasn't murdered. You told me she jumped to her death."

"Something Angus said to her that day persuaded her to leave her newborn baby and walk off that cliff."

"That's ludicrous! You're telling me Angus killed Andrew's wife, with a word, no less? Just whispered something that made her jump off the cliff? More than likely the poor woman suffered from postpartum depression."

"I'm telling you he killed them all, starting with Andrew's mother-in-law, the first Elizabeth."

"Why? Why would he do that? The successful baron you told me about doesn't sound like a maniacal killer." Duncan was insane if he thought she would believe Angus had beaten a woman to death, or had ever murdered anyone. "How did Livy and Betty die?" she asked in spite of herself.

"Livy and her daughter were swimming off a small boat on a lake in New York. They both went under and didn't surface. Their bodies were found entangled in thick water weeds in only four feet of water. The boat owner, a man they had hired for the day, disappeared before anyone could question him."

"What a horrible accident. They all died such violent deaths. I'm sorry I asked. Please, Duncan. Please, I don't want to hear any more. You can't come here and do this to me."

"It was no accident. You are not taking this as well as I had hoped."

"Wha—what? You expected me to take this—this horrifying story well?"

"I certainly expected to convince you of the danger you are in. "

"How many times do I have to tell you to get out? I want you gone." She stamped her foot and pointed angrily towards the front door. "Now!"

"As you wish," he said. "I'll go, but I will be back after you've had time to consider what I've told you. Think about it. Go over it again and again. It's important."

"Don't come back, Duncan. I mean it. I never want to see you again."

Without warning he gave her a searing kiss. Its intensity, and the immense relief that he was going to go away, almost buckled her knees.

"I will return," he promised. "You have a lot to think about so I will give you some time, but not much. I can't let him have you, too."

She stared at him. His kiss, albeit unwelcome, had brought back her longing for a substantial relationship. For a moment Elizabeth wished with all her heart that this attractive man with his twisted mind was normal. But he wasn't. He had fixated on his dead wife's family and created a horror story of their history. Now he was trying to shove his hallucinations down her throat.

If she allowed him to continue that would make her as twisted as he. "Oh, Duncan," she said wearily. "Even if your story was true, Angus wouldn't want to kill me. I'm not descended from Elizabeth Grayson."

"Think, Elizabeth, how did you come to own this house?"

"It was an inheritance from my Aunt Marguerite and Uncle Jasper. They died in an accident a little over three years ago."

"Marguerite was Beth's mother. You should study your family history."

"Beth?" Her hand flew to her mouth. "Oh, no! My cousin Beth was your wife?" Elizabeth sat with a thump and dropped her head into her hands. "She wasn't murdered, Duncan. She fell down a flight of stairs." She started crying. "It was a horrible accident. I've always regretted not being able to attend her funeral."

Elizabeth had been in the hospital mending from her boyfriend's latest temper tantrum. It was Beth's death that had made her realize how precious life was and had given her the initiative to leave Bobby.

"I didn't recognize her from the photos—the ones of her alive." She couldn't believe this. Duncan was her dead cousin's husband. "The last time I saw her she was ten and I was twelve. No one ever told me how it happened. Do you know?"

"She plunged a knife into her heart," Duncan said. "But Angus held her hand."

"You're insane." She dashed the tears from her eyes. "You knew who I was before you met me."

"I did."

"You could have told me the truth."

"I did. I haven't spoken one untrue thing to you."

"You claimed you didn't know me."

"I called you by name."

Indeed he had. And the forewarning she'd felt at the time was ignored. "I inherited this house because Beth died. My aunt and uncle had no other children. If they had died before Beth, you would own this house." Her heart slammed with alarm. "Is that why you came here? To get this house? Are you trying to frighten me into leaving?"

"Of course not. I wouldn't want this desolate property."

"Desolate?"

"I didn't mean that the way it sounded. It's just that this house is too big and empty for a single person, and too far from civilization to suit me." He tipped her face to his with a finger to her jaw. "But it suits you. You must believe me when I tell you thoughts of owning this house never entered my mind. It's you I am here for," he said. "I'm sorry to be so insistent, but there's very little time. I'm determined to stop Angus from killing again. If I am to save your life, I must have your cooperation, Elizabeth. You have to promise to read that diary."

"I'm not going to promise you anything because I don't believe you."

"Then I am going to have to persuade you."

"Please, go, Duncan. You said you would, and I honestly can't take anymore persuasion right now." She almost pushed him out the door, all the while hoping she wouldn't anger him.

She bolted the door behind him and stood there long after he left. How could she keep him from coming back? He had compromised her secure, comfortable life and left her badly frightened. Of him, she told herself, not Angus. Never Angus.

Elizabeth paced the floor, impatient for Angus to make himself known. She tried to make him come to her through the force of her will. It didn't work.

Duncan said her home was desolate. She studied the room, trying to see it through unfamiliar eyes. He was wrong. Desolation implied a lack of life. She looked at the seascape over the marble mantle. It took no imagination at all to see the painted waves roll and crash in cadence with the incessant sounds echoing up from the cliffs. The painting was alive. Every part of this house was alive. The most insignificant piece of molding, the flocked wallpaper, creaking plumbing and flickering converted gaslights all had a life force — one she had felt from the beginning.

Angus never came. Midnight crept up on her, and she was still too wide-awake to think about sleep. She would be exhausted at work tomorrow.

With nothing to do that would stop the workings of her mind, she took the diary and curled in the chair. Perhaps she could find something that would prove Duncan was wrong.

She turned the diary over and over in her hands. The cover was padded and covered in what must have once been lush wine velvet. The fabric was now thin, hard and rust-colored. The lock was broken. The inscription on the cover said simply, *Diary*. It could have been anyone's diary.

She brought me news the child was a girl. She seemed frail and unhappy as we stood in each other's arms on the balcony outside my bedroom. Spray from the surf pounding below rose up on the wind and soaked us. My desire to kill her was more potent than my desire to possess her had ever been. I wanted to throw her from the heights, to see her broken body dragged out to sea. Instead, I let her go, reliving my fantasy long into the night.

Duncan wanted her to believe these were Angus's own words. He wanted to convince her Angus's spirit returned repeatedly to fulfill his fantasies. The story was too bizarre to believe.

She closed the diary and held it in her lap. Her eyes were getting grainy. Lethargy stole over her. If she didn't get up soon and go to bed she would fall asleep in the chair.

The sound of wet glass shattering in the kitchen jolted her. *The lilies.*

"He lies about one thing and tells the truth about the other."

Elizabeth stood, dropping the diary on the floor. Her flesh crawled. "Angus?"

"You danced with him. You let him kiss you."

"You were watching," she accused. "Why didn't I feel your presence?"

"You weren't receptive to me." His voice was gravely, like it hadn't been used in a very long time. "You were open to him, to his suggestions, his aura, and his caresses. But you wanted me."

"I'm sure you know I've wanted you since the day I became aware of you."

"You were testing yourself."

"Yes." The word was released on a rush of air. Let him believe what he would.

Music, forlorn and exotic filled the room. Her candles burst into sparking flames. Angus was obviously pleased.

The scent of roses overrode the pervasive scent of the lilies, warning her of his impending ardor. She picked up the diary and held it out. "Is this yours?"

The music ceased with a discordant crash. The

candles went out, along with the electric lamp, plunging her into total darkness.

"Can you think of nothing else to do when I displease you?"

She turned on the overhead light in the kitchen and studied the disaster on the floor. Her mouth tightened as she cleaned up the broken vase and spilled water. She would have been happy to throw the lilies away, but she defiantly shoved the bruised flowers into a plastic pitcher and added water. Let him break that.

"I need some answers, Angus." She started washing the dishes she'd left in the sink. "All you're concerned about is how I feel about you. I really thought you cared for me. How can you let that man say all those horrible things about you and yet refuse to defend yourself?"

Angrily she slammed one of the goblets on the counter. Suds flew. The stem snapped. A chip of glass drew blood on the edge of her hand. She sucked it. "People's feelings get hurt when they hear bad things about the ones they love. Don't you remember that from your own life? You know I love you. You know I don't believe a single word he said, but if you care at all you would want to comfort me."

She made her way to bed, wishing she had a living, breathing roommate. Some nights were not meant to be spent alone. Especially one at the end of the kind of day this had been.

Yet, if she could keep Angus from her bed tonight by

the force of her will, she would.

Chapter **13**

Elizabeth had to find out the truth. She set aside
her misgivings and tried to Google Angus Aberdeen the
next evening. No sooner did she enter his name in the
search bar than her laptop froze. She slammed it shut with
relief, deciding the chore would best be done at work, in
the light of day, surrounded by people and away from
Angus.

It was another week before she found the courage and
privacy to try again in her office. There was scant
information online. What there was proved Angus had
indeed been an influential person both in Midville and in

Congress. His demise was alluded to as an unfortunate incident involving an intruder, which resulted in his death. Not one photograph or portrait was to be found.

There was absolutely nothing about the Graysons. Duncan had most likely made up the story about Andrew and his wife.

She had always assumed no one other than she knew of the existence of Angus's spirit. But surely his presence in the house had been instrumental in its lack of long-term tenants. Had her aunt and uncle known about him? They must have. How else could Duncan have found out?

What drove him to investigate Angus's history and then weave such a complex scenario that spanned generations? She could almost understand how anguish over his beloved wife's death could have driven him to the brink of insanity. But Duncan seemed to have topped over that edge. He should be getting past his initial grief and trying to rebuild his life. Instead he was obsessed with her ghost . . . and her.

She tried to recall what she had known about her cousin. Her memories stopped when they were young. She had never been close to Beth, who lived so far away. She had spent a few weeks with her aunt and uncle one summer; and had played with Beth's paper dolls for hours on end while Beth ran off to play with her friends. They hadn't liked each other enough to maintain contact when they grew up.

She vaguely recalled hearing about Beth's marriage.

She tried to imagine Duncan with the disinterested, selfish girl her cousin had been, and felt a burst of irrational anger that she had left so much pain behind.

As soon as she got home she phoned her mother. They spent several minutes chatting about inconsequential things before she found the nerve to ask about her cousin. "Mom, I was thinking about Beth today. How did she die?"

"We told you. She fell down the cellar stairs."

"I seem to recall someone had mentioned a knife?" Her mother was silent for so long Elizabeth wondered if she'd hung up. "Mom?"

"Why are you bringing this up?"

"Is there some reason you don't want to tell me?"

"She fell on a knife," her mother finally said.

"She was carrying a knife when she fell?" Elizabeth's pulse skittered. "What really happened?"

Her mother's deep breath was audible over the phone. "We thought, because of your condition, it might be best not to tell you. I'm so sorry."

"Tell me now."

"The fall didn't kill her. She'd been stabbed and was dead before she hit the cellar floor."

"Who stabbed her?"

"You know the coroner said her death was an accident. There were some who suggested her husband killed her."

"What do you think?"

"Elizabeth . . ."

"I'm not the same person anymore. I can handle the truth."

"I can't believe she fell on the knife several times like that. Once, maybe, but over and over, each time in a different place? It doesn't seem possible."

"Could she have done it on purpose?"

"No. It took tremendous strength to--to do so much damage. Besides, she had no reason to want to die. She was happy. She confided in Marguerite that she was going to talk to her husband about starting a family."

"What was her husband's name?"

"Duncan. Duncan Munroe."

Elizabeth swallowed the lump that rose in her throat. A buzzing began in her ears. "I know was in a bad place. I know you wanted to protect me, but mom, you should have told me."

"We made the best decision we could at the time, honey. I can't go back and change it. What difference does it make now?"

It made all the difference in the world. It gave macabre credence to Duncan's story. It also made her realize she was right to be afraid of him. "I take it you think her husband killed her."

"Oh, no. Absolutely not! That poor man had nothing at all to do with Beth's death. He was inconsolable. We all thought he might die of his pain, or kill himself." Her mother's voice broke. "He found her, you know. The next day, when Marguerite came to take Beth shopping she found them in the cellar. He had been cradling her body all night. They had to inject him with a sedative so they could take her away."

"Oh, mom, that's terrible." Elizabeth squeezed her eyes tight against her tears. She couldn't conceive of such devotion. It certainly wasn't the behavior of a murderer. "So you think it was an accident?"

"No, I don't. I think she was killed by an intruder. I think whoever it was had to be very angry, and very powerful. I can't imagine anyone hating that lovely girl enough to do that to her."

"But the police and coroner didn't there was foul play?"

"They claimed there was no sign of a struggle, no sign of forced entry and the doors had been bolted at the time of her death. Hers were the only fingerprints on the knife and on, well, anything, and they checked thoroughly. They found no evidence or DNA. The thing is it wasn't her knife. I never saw it but I heard it was very old and had an antler handle. According to Marguerite, Beth never owned anything like it. We'll never know the truth."

"I suppose not." Elizabeth felt lightheaded. "Mom, I'm not feeling so great. I'll call you next week. Give my love to daddy." She hung up and ran to the bathroom where she vomited.

An image of Duncan cradling his dead wife remained emblazoned in Elizabeth's brain. She thought of nothing else for days. She felt remorse for having been frightened by him. He had never raised a hand or his voice to her. His touches were affectionate and his words full of care and concern. He was simply a miserable man who was seeking consolation and closure. Unfortunately, he was going about it the wrong way.

She wanted to tell Angela and Christy about him but there was no way to explain why he had appeared in her life without telling them about Angus.

She found she wanted to see him again and do something to make his sadness disappear. She felt compelled to nurture and soothe him the way she had every other man with whom she had been involved. But this was different. She wasn't involved with him. Not that way. She ignored the tiny voice in her head that said, "*Not yet . . .*"

Although her fear was gone, she still resented his behavior. If he ever returned he would have some apologizing to do.

She thought about Duncan so much it began to border on obsession. He exuded a thrilling power, at odds with his soothing voice and gentle manners. He was definitely not the type of man who usually drew her interest.

But then again, neither was Angus.

The less she thought of Angus, the more he insidiously crept into her space. He wrote ancient script in the steam on her bathroom mirror. He hid her things: her favorite jewelry, her hairbrush, even the novel she was reading. Her milk soured in the refrigerator. He woke her from sleep by slamming cupboard doors.

He was trying to get her attention. She couldn't stay angry with him. In fact, she felt flattered to know she had enough power to cause him even a little of the chagrin he sometimes made her feel. Besides, she was lonely. It was a waste of time mooning over Duncan. It was time to put him behind her and concentrate on her ghostly lover.

That evening Elizabeth bathed, washed her hair and shaved her body as if preparing for a human paramour. She massaged her skin with warm, rose-scented oil. "Angus," she called softly. "I think we should start anew. Let's forget Duncan ever came here. I want our old life back."

She knew Angus agreed when he melted over her like warm wax. He drew her to the bed and entered her body in ways a mortal man never could. An unearthly passion removed her core being from her body and sent it spinning through the universe.

It was a long time before she came to her worldly senses.

Life did not return to the way it had been. Angus taught her what it was like to live on the pinnacle of desire. She couldn't get enough of him, and he apparently couldn't get enough of her.

He drove her to the heights of heaven and the depths of hell with his lovemaking. Night after night they joined in glorious fusion. She awoke from those nights fatigued and hollow-eyed.

Day after day, Elizabeth went through the motions at the office. She became increasingly distracted and withdrawn. She stopped going out to lunch with her friends. At the end of each workday she was exhausted and anxious to return home so Angus could bring her to life again.

She lost weight. The quality of her work declined until Mr. Clark noticed and called her into his office.

"Sit down, please," he said. "Elizabeth, you are one of my best employees. You're an asset to this company--an asset to me. I don't mean to pry but I feel like there might be something wrong. Is there anything you'd like to talk about?" He reached across the desk and took her hand. "Anything I can help you with?"

She had expected a reprimand, not a show of concern. But then again, what did she know to expect from this middle-aged, soft-spoken man? For the most part he left his employees to run the office and seldom intruded on their daily routine. She forced a smile. "I've been having trouble sleeping lately. Other than that, everything is fine."

"If you have, er, financial problems--"

"No. Really," she interjected, removing her hand from his and rising. "I'm sorry I've been so distracted lately. I know it has been affecting my work. I'll rest more and even see a doctor if I can't get past this bout of insomnia." She stood there, uncertainly, hoping he would take the hint and dismiss her.

The potent, musky aroma of sex suddenly filled the room. Angus! Shocked and humiliated, she wanted to run-- to get away from her boss before he smelled it. "I-I really sh-should get back to my work."

His concerned expression slid into something else-- something calculating and greedy. He rose and walked around the desk. His gaze dropped in slow increments from her face to her twisting hands, to her feet, and then slowly rose back to her face. "Please let me know if you need anything." His smooth voice had turned rough. "Anything at all."

She turned from him and almost ran out of his office. "How dare you?" she raged at Angus. "How dare you follow me here?"

"Liz?" Angela blocked her way to the restroom. "Who were you talking to?"

Everyone was staring at her. She'd spoken out loud, the way she usually communicated with Angus. The habit had become ingrained. Now that she knew he wasn't confined to their home she was going to have to be very careful.

"No one followed you. Mr. Clark is still in his office." Angela grabbed Elizabeth's arm and dragged her into a cubicle near the hall. "What happened in there? Why were you yelling at him?"

"I wasn't yelling at Mr. Clark. Nothing happened. I was just thinking about something and I spoke out loud."

"You sounded upset. He didn't fire you, did he?"

"No! He just wanted to know if I was okay. He asked if I needed anything."

"That's all he said?"

"He told me he was concerned. He said if I had problems he would help in any way he could."

"We all feel that way. You haven't been yourself in a while. I think you may be depressed. You should see a doctor."

"You think I need to see a psychiatrist?"

"That's not what I meant and you know it. There are several medical reasons for depression."

"I'm not depressed. I'm not unhappy or stressed. I'm just tired. Other than that, I'm fine."

"You don't look fine. You look ill and you're acting paranoid. Are you afraid of something?" She reached out and tentatively touched Elizabeth's shoulder. "You know you can talk to me."

No, she couldn't. She couldn't conceive of telling Angela or anyone about the pleasure and euphoria she received from a ghost. She couldn't tell her about the craving she had for him, about the arousal that ambushed her at the mere thought of him. The fact everything else in life was becoming unimportant in comparison to Angus was something she had to keep to herself.

She couldn't tell her she suspected her growing passion provided Angus the means to follow her beyond the house on Mulberry Drive.

For a split second, she wished she could talk to Angela. If only she could tell her about her ever-increasing desires and her powerlessness to control them. "I'm tired. I just need a vacation. I haven't had one in three years."

Since moving in with Angus she had taken only occasional days off. She'd been content to spend her time at home with him and hadn't wanted to go anywhere else. "I'm going to ask Mr. Clark if I can take a month off." The sudden idea struck her as ideal. She would have a month to spend with her lover, a month to set some ground rules in their relationship—and a month to forget the hunger in Mr. Clark's eyes.

Her vexation with Angus was gone, replaced by the anticipation of spending day and night with him. "I need the time off. I'm sorry if this is going to be a problem."

"I'm sure it won't be," Angela insisted. "We managed before you came. We'll manage without you for a while."

Elizabeth knew it would be difficult for her friends to take up her slack at work. She would make it up to them someday. "Christy won't be happy."

"Christy is as worried about you as I am. She'll be okay with this. I'm certain Mr. Clark will be, too. Will you go to visit your parents?"

"I—I—haven't thought about it, but, yes, probably." Her face felt hot from the lie.

"Good."

Angela's worried look shamed Elizabeth.

Chapter **14**

The next few days passed in a haze of lust and love. Elizabeth tossed and writhed on sheets made damp with passion. She didn't eat. She seldom slept.

Angus finally took pity and left her alone. She knew from her sensitized emotions he didn't go far, but he didn't touch her.

She bathed and rested and summoned up the energy to make a pot of potato cheddar soup, tidying her bedroom as it simmered. She took a nap, ate and then did the dishes.

When the sun started to go down she bundled up, put on her boots and went outside. The air in her home seemed stale and musty. The crisp air outside was like a rebirth. Everything was covered with a powdery white blanket of new snow. Her house was too, except for the roof where there were melted patches by the chimney.

This was her favorite time to walk the grounds. The harsh light of day exposed too much: Rotting sills, missing shingles, peeling paint. Twilight painted a pastel haze over the house like blush on a woman's cheeks. Her house was old. Like an old woman, it was best viewed in flattering light.

She walked the path that ran alongside the house from the front to the back. Snow muffled the sound of gravel crunching under her feet. As she rounded the back corner she trailed her fingers over the boxwood hedge that hugged the foundation, sending glittering snowflakes spinning on the wind. They drifted onto her face like frozen fairy kisses.

She went to the edge of the promontory and looked down. Far below, rolling waves turned into hollow booms as the water exploded upon the rocks. A frigid wind blew across the boiling waters of the sea. Vapors rose like wisps of steam. A dense fog shrouded the moon.

At times like this it was easy to imagine she was the only living person in the world. The fog enveloped her like Angus did. She could escape the fog, but not him. Not even out here where she'd come to clear thoughts of him from her mind. He held her captive. He would never release her from that bond. Nor would he allow her to break it.

The wind was sharp enough to be painful. Elizabeth ducked beneath the balcony that overlooked the sea. She raised her gaze to the substructure of the balcony. It looked like a skeleton in the weak light. Made of wood, it ran the length of the back of the house. It extended out from the exterior wall about twelve feet, almost to the point where the earth abruptly cascaded to the rocks a hundred feet below. She stood beneath the portion closest to the cliff. Was this where Andrew's wife had jumped to her doom?

She closed her eyes. It felt like she was suspended in air. When she opened them she peered intently but couldn't see over the cliff. The delineation between lawn and sky had disappeared in the fog. She shivered. If she took five steps . . . or maybe six . . . or seven . . .

A sound—not the sea, not Angus, who had never followed her outside—had her looking around. Unnerved, she fisted her frozen hands, one over the other, and blew hot breath against her thumbs, through her knit gloves. This was ridiculous. She was imagining things. Then it came again, once more from behind her.

Spinning, she came face to face with Duncan.

Her laughter, a reflex reaction to her foolish fear, died in her throat. "Where on earth did you come from?"

"I came from around the other side of the house," he said.

"No," she protested. The fog suddenly dissipated.

Her pristine lawn now appeared silver in the moonlight. There were no tracks to indicate the direction from which Duncan had come. "I would have seen you."

"I noticed you. Your head was down. You seemed lost in reverie. You weren't expecting me, thus you didn't look for me."

He was right. She had not been looking for him, or anyone. If he had come from the other side of the house he must have been here awhile watching her, because the wind obviously had had enough time to dust over his footprints with snow.

"Am I disturbing you? I'll leave if you want."

"I'm not happy you are here, Duncan. I think you should go."

"I will, I promise, as soon as I tell you how sorry I am." He removed his hat, the same way he had when she'd first met him. "I'm a good person, Elizabeth. I am not the kind of man who hurts others without remorse. I sincerely regret causing you distress. I was so intent on telling you about Angus, I didn't realize I was frightening you."

"You knew," she accused. "You didn't care."

"I cared more than you can imagine. I care now. That's why I'm here."

There was no doubting his sincerity. He exuded the same plaintive aura that had persuaded her to allow him into her home and her life. She tamped down dregs of resentment and found herself glad he had come. She suddenly wanted to touch his hair and run the tips of her gloved fingers over his face. She wanted to bring light to his dark, watchful eyes. A need to nurture this broken man bloomed in her heart—a need to give that which she had never received.

Her stomach clenched with guilt. She would bet Angus knew her thoughts, even out here in the frozen winter air.

"Let's go inside," she offered.

"Not yet. That house is Angus's domain. I have things to say to you I don't want to share with him."

She tightened her mouth. "Are we going to go there again?"

"You can deny being aware Angus Aberdeen dwells in your home," Duncan said. "But I know the truth. I feel him when he is there. I know when he is not. And I know you are lying."

"What brings you here, Duncan?" she snapped. She was upset for having been happy to see him again. "Never mind, I don't care. I'm freezing. I'm going in. You're welcome to come with me, but I'm not staying out here to chat."

"After you," he said, with an old-fashioned bow and a gesture with his hat.

She immediately regretted her invitation. Angus had been in a delightful mood lately. If Duncan came inside she would have to make certain they spoke of nothing that would upset him.

Duncan stomped the snow off his boots before stepping through the front door. He hung his coat on the hall tree and put his hat on the sideboard.

She stuffed her gloves into her pockets and removed her coat and scarf. She hung them next to his. The simply, intimate act made her heart ache.

They stood in her foyer, studying each other.

"You look different," he murmured.

She blushed, knowing what he saw in her that wasn't there before.

"You look like a woman in love."

That wasn't what she had expected him to say. And there was no reply she could make. She still hadn't admitted the existence of Angus to Duncan.

He made no attempt to move from the entrance hall into the house. "You have snow in your hair," he said, brushing it lightly, letting his hand linger.

"Oh," she said, "the boxwood . . ." Her chagrin fled. Her mouth went dry at the look on his face.

"Elizabeth," he groaned. His need, his longing, they were there in his eyes.

Warmth slowly radiated through her body. Her breath quickened in anticipation. So he had been reluctant to come inside because he desired her and didn't want Angus to know. That was why he had returned.

The tug on her heart turned into a pull as strong as the moon's on the tide and all because she could see his eyes. Oh, his very blue, very *alive* eyes . . .

She couldn't break contact with his gaze. She stroked his jaw and lightly brushed his lips with her fingers before she was aware she had moved.

Touching him made her sizzle inside. It felt like the aftereffects of a bolt of lightning. She wanted him. This crazy man, obsessed with his wife's death. This man with whom she was still angry. She wanted him. No doubt her desire was as evident to him as his was to her.

He caught her hand, kissing her palm with his warm, human lips. His breath, hot and wet, sent rivers of need coursing through her.

Oh, yes, she belonged to Angus, but what an unfair advantage this living man held over him.

His mouth moved lazily across the sensitive skin of her temple. She threw back her head as his kiss trailed down to the indentation at the base of her throat. She became aware that the moans filling her ears were her own.

Duncan was playing off all the new sensations she had developed, all the hunger that filled her to overflowing. She was completely at his mercy.

Right or wrong suddenly had no meaning to her anymore. Her fidelity to Angus spun away like rising sparks from a fire. She needed Angus; she wanted Duncan. She couldn't make a choice between them. She wouldn't.

She wrapped her arms around Duncan's neck and slipped to the floor, taking him with her.

If Angus was watching, she no longer cared.

Hours later, Elizabeth lay in bed watching Duncan breathe as he slept. She studied the rise and fall of his chest, the very realism of his features. There was nothing of him left to her imagination.

She held her hand close to his arm. His skin was tanned, hers was pale. His hands were large. Hers were delicate. It was a heady feeling indeed to know she was capable of giving Duncan the same kind of joy he had brought her. She was overjoyed to be a woman.

With Angus, she was always shaken to find herself in the bondage of a body.

Chapter <u>15</u>

Although she tried not to think of Duncan while she was inside her home, Elizabeth often found herself ambushed with arousal when she remembered her last hours with him. She often went for walks, seeking privacy from Angus in which to relive Duncan's lovemaking and anticipate his return.

Days passed, but he didn't come back to her. He didn't answer his cell phone. Her pride wouldn't let her seek him at the Lighthouse Inn. For all she knew he had left Midville.

Perhaps he had used her. Perhaps he had preyed upon her perceived loneliness. It didn't matter. She wasn't in love with him. She had been as much of a seductress as he had been a seducer. If she never saw him again, she would always have that one precious day.

Angus made certain she was aware that he knew of her simmering passion for Duncan. Her ghost lover's outrage and anger took its toll. Her nights were full of torment. Angus made love to her until she thought she would die from the exquisite sensations. Afterwards, exhausted, she would fall into deeply troubled sleep where nightmares relentlessly haunted her.

Her dreams were of death and torture, wailing and screaming. She dreamed she was bludgeoned, burned, drowned and stabbed. Every morning she awoke to the odor of burning flesh.

"Enough," she begged. "Will you punish me forever?" She had bruises on her arms and legs. Bite marks on her breasts. Her hair had turned lank and dry. Her skin was chapped.

She lost track of time, drifting from hour to hour and day to day. She no longer dressed in the morning. What was the point? No living person had seen her in weeks.

She refused to answer her cell phone or check her voice mail. She feared Angela would call and question her, or worse, want to visit. Finally, she turned it completely off. Her television remained cold and silent. Her laptop went unused. Nothing that went on in the world was of interest to her.

She forced herself to fan out the stack of mail on the hall sideboard. It had fallen through the door slot with regularity over the past few weeks and she'd carelessly scooped it up and tossed it, with little interest, into the copper pot.

What she held in her hand was mostly bills and some catalogues. She started when she saw a second electric bill. The postmark was exactly one month from the other that was still unopened. With a little nip of fright, she realized she had to arouse herself enough to pay her bills before she wound up having services cut. It would be hell, living in this place without electricity.

A letter from her mother caught her attention. She had promised to call her, and then had forgotten. She started to put it on the stack of four that were still unopened. She hesitated. This one would go in the fire, unread. It was too thin to be one of her mother's chatty letters. Surely it was a reprimand or demand. She didn't want to be tempted to call or write. Her mother sensed too much and worried too much. That worry was a burden. She would contact her when she returned to work and this interlude was over.

Work! Her heart slammed. Mr. Clark had given her permission to take a month off. Vacation time she'd earned, and deserved. But surely more than a month had passed. She had made herself unavailable. He would be furious. Did she still have a job?

She found her cell phone beneath a stack of unread newspapers piled on the kitchen counter. It was completely discharged. She rummaged through the drawers for her charger, plugged it into the phone and sat at the table, feet tucked up and arms around her knees, watching it.

She should be hungry. She might be if she had bread to make a sandwich, or produce to make a salad. The canned goods, all that was left of her food supply, had lost their appeal. Nevertheless, when she summoned up enough energy to move, she would open a can of something.

How many minutes had passed? She snapped the cord from her phone and pressed the power button, waiting impatiently for it to load. It was charged enough to make a call, but there were no bars. She went from room to room, holding it against windows with no success. Granted, the stone and tin of her house reduced the strength of her provider's radio waves, but she had always had adequate service.

She rechecked the pile of mail in the hall. It contained a cell phone bill three weeks old. Not enough time had passed to get a new bill, yet alone a disconnect notice. She worried her bottom lip between her teeth. Angus. He was behind this. Her beloved was jealous of anything that took her mind off him.

Now she would have to get dressed and go to the agency to face her employer. She looked up from the mail into the Baroque mirror. When had she gotten those dark smudges beneath her eyes? She blew her breath into her hand, not remembering if she had brushed her teeth this morning.

The door chime made her jump. She choked back a scream. *Duncan*. No. She couldn't let him see her like this. And if he made Angus angry, there would be hell for her to pay. She held her breath as if the person beyond the door could hear her.

"Liz!" The word was sharp and spoke of panic.

It was Angela.

Angela twisted the bell handle and called her name again. "Liz, are you there?"

Elizabeth turned hot with humiliation. She still wore her stained nightgown. Her hair was a snarled mess. She looked down at her bare feet and noticed glass shards on the floor, missed by the broom, mixed with dust. Some had dried blood on them. She should have swept them up weeks ago.

Angela pounded the ancient oak door. She frantically twisted the bell handle. "I'm coming in." The door knob rattled but the lock held.

Angela had seen her fetch the key from the mouth of the garden gargoyle by the boxwoods. Elizabeth knew if she didn't answer, her friend would come in anyway. She flipped the lock and opened the door.

"Oh!" Obviously startled, Angela stared at her for a few seconds. She put her hand to her mouth and averted her eyes. "Your--your hair has grown." When she looked back at Elizabeth there was censure and confusion in her expression. "I've called you a dozen times. You won't answer. You don't call me back. What's going on?"

"My cell phone has been acting up. I seldom check it anymore. I'm sorry."

"Why haven't you called me? It's been weeks. You should be back at work by now."

"I'm sorry." Elizabeth pushed her hair back as well as she could with her arms crossed at her chest. Her nightgown was all but transparent. Not that it mattered. Her breasts had become so small she no longer needed a bra.

"What have you been doing, alone out here, all this time?"

"Housework, laundry, reading. It's been nice, working around the house in my nightclothes, not having to get dressed and go out in this nasty weather."

"What nasty weather? It's cold but it has been sunny for days." Angela crossed her arms and took a stance. She clearly had no intentions of leaving.

Elizabeth stood aside. "Come on in." She let Angela lead the way down the entrance hall, through the parlor and into the kitchen.

Angela wrinkled her nose. "Something smells terrible in here." She scanned the room and then headed for the pantry. Inside, the wastepaper can was overflowing. Garbage was mixed in with papers and dry trash. She scooped up a mess on the floor and stuffed it into the can.

When she opened the back door to set it outside, sunlight stabbed Elizabeth's eyes with a brilliance that made her blink. A rush of fresh air diluted the odor of decay that suddenly seemed overwhelming. An odor she hadn't noticed before.

"You should leave the door open for a while," Angela said. "Let it air out in here." She glanced around the kitchen. Her mouth formed a slight twist of distaste as she snapped on the overhead light. "Mr. Clark is concerned. He's been trying to get in touch with you."

"I'm sorry. Can you tell him my cell phone has been acting up?"

"Okay." The word was spoken with hesitation. "He asked me to apologize for any misunderstanding that day in his office. I don't know what happened between the two of you, and you obviously don't want to tell me, but he thinks you quit. I promised you didn't."

Elizabeth flushed at the implied reprimand. "I just lost track of time. I'm ready to come back to work immediately. In fact, I was getting ready to get dressed when you showed up. I'm going into the office this afternoon to let him know I'll be back full time, starting tomorrow."

"This afternoon? It's after five. The office is closed."

After five? It seemed like she had just gotten out of bed. "Oh, I—I didn't realize it was so late." Angela must think she had lost her mind. "I've been reading." It was a weak excuse and did nothing to erase the concern on

153

Angela's face. "I'm sorry I haven't kept in better touch. I really have been busy catching up on chores around here. How have you been?"

"I'm pregnant."

Chapter **16**

Elizabeth sat at the kitchen table across from her friend. Her focus was on her bare feet. They were chilled against the soapstone floor. "I'm sorry, Angela. I don't remember what he looked like." In truth, Elizabeth hadn't paid attention to either of the men the girls had picked up that night in Damon's. That Angela's fling had turned into a real affair was startling and enviable.

"He's beautiful," Angela sighed. She'd popped the top on a can of soda, all that Elizabeth had to offer. She didn't drink it, yet seemed intrigued by the can. She studied it, running a finger around the rim. "And he is ecstatic about the baby." Condensation turned into beads of water that worked their way slowly down the aluminum can. Angela made a show of sopping the moisture off the porcelain surface with a tissue she'd pulled from her purse.

Elizabeth wished she had put on a bathrobe when she'd gotten out of bed this morning. "I'm going upstairs to get dressed," she said. If you would rather have something warm to drink, there's a canister of coffee by the coffeemaker. You could start a pot if you'd like. I won't be long."

Elizabeth rummaged around in her closet. She didn't own a single pair of jeans that would stay up around her slim hips. She chose what had been her tightest pair and snaked a braided leather belt through the loops, cinching it to the last hole. The denim gathered like a skirt around her waist.

Her favorite sweater, a silky pink pullover, hung like a sheet on her. It exposed too much. She pulled a sweat shirt over it. She had once worn it to paint her bedroom. It still had blue stains on the sleeves. So what? It was only Angela. And the layers were bulky enough to hide her protruding bones.

Her friend was going to have a baby. She ran her hands down her own concave belly. It was all happening so fast. Or perhaps it was simply that time had stood still for her for so long she could barely comprehend the changes going on in Angela's life.

Her stomach knotted. Her friend was down there alone, but not alone. Angus was very present and she sensed he didn't like Angela being in the house. It didn't matter. This was her home, not his.

She slid her feet into black suede moccasins, the first shoes she'd worn in days. As soft as they were, they felt abrasive to her tender feet. There was nothing she could do about her hair except run a brush through the lank strands.

Angela was waiting in the parlor. She had put her coat back on and wound her scarf around her throat. It was the scarf Elizabeth had given to her for Christmas, along with a pair of lemon-jade earrings the same buttery yellow shade.

Angela had her hand to her mouth and was staring at a maze of spider webs and water stains on the ceiling. She had pulled the curtains to the sides of the windows.

Elizabeth was mortified to realize the glass panes were smeared with greasy soot from the fireplace. Dust motes floated in the sun rays that exposed the room like candles and the dark-jeweled chandelier never had.

Angela made a choking sound.

"I guess I should air this room out, too."

Angela spun to face her. "Oh! You startled me. I'm just allergic to dust."

Elizabeth grasped the bottom of a window and tugged. It wouldn't budge.

"Don't bother with that, Liz. I'm leaving."

"You don't want coffee? I'll make it. Maybe I have

some cookies or something."

"No. I really don't want anything, and I have things to do on my way home. I just came to make certain you were okay." She hugged herself. "It's warmer outside than it is in here." Her expression was guarded. "There's something else. I'm not sure I want to drop it on you like this, but I haven't seen or heard from you in so long, and I couldn't get in touch with you. I'm getting married." She said it softly, with a smile.

Guilt for having been so unapproachable was like blow to Elizabeth's heart. "Married? But you just met him." Elizabeth remembered her careless remark about Angela sending her rejected boyfriends her way. She would laugh if she didn't feel so pathetic.

"I know, but I feel as if we've been together forever. I love him, Liz and he loves me. This time I am sure. We're thinking around the end of May, or early June."

Angela's joy was so potent Elizabeth could feel it. "That's a beautiful time of year for a wedding," she said. "I'm so happy for you."

"We have to fatten you up. I want you to be my maid of honor."

Elizabeth's vision blurred with tears. "I would love to." She stepped back when Angela moved. She should share this moment with a touch, a hug, but she felt too fragile and unclean. "My gosh. I can hardly believe so much has happened in such a short time."

"Life has been like the proverbial snowball." Angela's

hand went to her belly. "I missed sharing this with you."

"Have you picked out any names for the baby, yet?"

"No. It's too soon." She clutched her purse. "I have to go. You will be at work tomorrow?"

"I'll be there. Hopefully Mr. Clark will understand."

"Tell him you've been ill." She glanced at Elizabeth's frail wrists and then dropped her gaze to her legs. "You've lost so much weight he will believe you."

She leaned into Elizabeth and kissed her cheek before she could react. Her hand lightly swept her shoulder blade. "I almost believe it myself. I have this feeling of foreboding. Like something is terribly wrong. You can tell me anything, Liz. I'll help you if I can. I won't tell a soul what we talk about."

Elizabeth bit back her words. She was tempted to tell Angela everything. She needed her friend. She suspected she needed help. "I'm fine. I swear."

"If you don't come to work tomorrow, I'm coming back."

"I'll be there."

"I mean it, Liz. If you don't show up, I will return."

Chapter **17**

That night Angus bedeviled Elizabeth with a maelstrom of pleasure and pain that left her sleepless and aching. If his attentions had been relentless since Duncan left, they increased after Angela's visit.

When she could take no more, she slipped out of bed and went into the bathroom. She was exhausted and she didn't want to wait for the water to fill. She stepped into the old fashioned claw-foot bathtub and drew the shower curtain closed. The warm spray felt wonderful on the aches in her body. She soaped herself and let the water wash the suds away. Her head lolled back, her hair got wet. Now she would have to dry it or go to sleep with it wet. The thought made goose bumps rise, even in the warmth of the water.

She twisted the cold water faucet to off, then the hot water faucet. But the hot water handle wouldn't budge. The water turned scalding. She screeched and jumped away from the stream.

Her foot slipped and she was thrown against the far wall. Bracing her hand on the edge of the tub, she reached out to grasp the shower curtain. It snapped the hooks and flew at her, enveloping her in a prison of vinyl that sucked against her, forcing her upright and slamming her to the wall.

Panicking, she tried to claw at the curtain, but the harder she struggled, the more it sucked against her until she was totally immobile.

She couldn't turn her head. Each attempt to breathe drew the vinyl further into her mouth. Steaming water beat against the curtain and drummed in her ears. The unbearable heat was joined by pressure that slid from her neck to her thighs like a lover's hard hands.

Through the dense curtain her brain registered a darkness that fluttered like a rabid bat. The pressure increased, slipping from her breasts to her sex, and slipping beneath the vinyl to enter her very core.

A powerful orgasm jolted her. Her heart stopped, and then slammed with alarming pain.

She couldn't breathe. Black dots sparked in her vision. A buzzing in her brain grew louder and louder. *Angus!*

Angus! I'm dying!

Cold seeped into Elizabeth's consciousness. She jerked upright, gasping for air, unable to take in enough. She was naked and slick with sweat. The bed was soaked. The room was freezing. She sat up and rolled into a ball, hugging herself. She had no recollection of how she got to the bed.

The temperature in the bedroom suddenly rose like a blast from a furnace. She stopped shivering but couldn't shake the lingering embrace of terror. Tears ran down her face as she pulled in one deep breath after another. When her senses fully returned, she felt Angus's powerful aura of satisfaction. It made her nauseated. "You had no right," she croaked.

"Some people find the experience exquisite."

Elizabeth gasped at the rusty sound of his voice. "It wasn't exquisite. It was horrible and terrifying," she cried. Will you kill me?" Asphyxiation sex was something she would never have willingly participated in. "Are you trying to make me believe you could be the monster Duncan claims you are? Or are you simply jealous of a mortal man?"

The breaking surf, the soughing wind went silent for a moment, and then resumed in a rush. A shift in the air told her something she'd said had affected Angus. "Is that it? You're jealous of a living man?"

"Don't be deceived. Duncan is no more alive than I

am."

"That's not true, Angus. He's a man--a living, breathing human. I've touched him." Her skin grew hot with the memory.

"He is an apparition, my dear. He is dead, and deadly powerful. His force is stronger than mine. The evil deeds in his past life have given him a strength I could never hope to have. You must believe me. He wants you. And all I want is to protect you."

Something hot and frenzied dashed through her midsection, nauseating her. "Protect me? You almost killed me! You're lying about Duncan. He's not a ghost, and he would never hurt me. He is gentle and kind. He's never touched me in anger."

Angus's laugh was a hollow sound that sent chills down Elizabeth's spine. "Hurt you? That he would, and he could kill you without a thought, but it's not your body he is after. He wants your eternal soul."

Chapter **18**

Elizabeth got up the next morning feeling exhausted. Yesterday had been a day of mental and physical jolts. The night had been sleepless and full of turmoil. She had to find out the truth.

And the truth would only come from Duncan. All thoughts of going to see Mr. Clark flew right out of her mind.

She spent the morning trying to contact Duncan. He didn't answer his cell phone. The young-sounding agent at the Lighthouse Inn said she didn't know of any one by his name, but she had just started her job and it was possible he had checked out before. Elizabeth assumed he had left Midville and she would never have the chance to confront him.

The doorbell rang. A miasma of dread settled in as she approached the door.

Duncan stood there, his ever-present hat in hand, his hang-dog expression in place. How convenient that he'd chosen to return only after Angus's unbelievable accusation. "We need to talk," he said.

"After all this time, that is how you greet me?" She spun on her heel and stalked into the living room. He followed and she gestured for him to sit on the couch. She sat at the other end. "What do you want to talk about?"

"Beth—"

"Don't go there." She stiffened.

"All right," he said. "What do you want to talk about?"

"This isn't a friendly chit chat, Duncan. Say what you came to say."

"I missed you." He offered no excuses for having abandoned her. He didn't apologize for not contacting her.

"I'm sure you did." He was going to toy with her. Well, two could play that game. "Yes, Angus lives here," she abruptly admitted. "He told me you were evil. He told me you were a spirit and you wanted to harm me." If she had hoped to shock him, she was disappointed.

"Do you believe I am a spirit?"

"Of course not." Her nighttime fears seemed foolish

as she studied him. He was as real and alive as she.

"I would never do anything to harm you. It wounds me to the core to know you fear me."

His sad mien was the part of his persona that had first attracted her to him. It drew no sympathy from her now. She'd had experience with men who lied, then used their charm to make her believe those lies. "I have no way of knowing if you would harm me or not. I hardly know you. I do know I'm not afraid of you."

"You are," Duncan said, his gaze fixed on her hands.

They were clenched in her lap. Her knuckles were white. "You have no idea how I feel. Who are you? Why are you here? I deserve to know the truth."

"The truth is I am a spirit."

"No!" She thought for a moment the shock would kill her. "I don't believe you. What kind of cruel game is this?"

"It's no game, Elizabeth." He spoke her name with a long, drawn hiss. "You knew."

"I did not! I didn't."

"You did. You may not want to admit it, but that knowledge came to you when we met out there in the snow. That's why you couldn't wait to return to the house."

"What do you want with me? I didn't seek you out. I didn't seek Angus. Both of you came to me." She no longer thought either Angus or Duncan loved her. She felt like a pawn in a cruel game. If only she had never answered the door that day.

Duncan slid close to her. "And now you will know

the whole of it," he said. "Angus and I have a horrifying, entwined history. We are bound to each other until one of us breaks free. "He gently pressed her to his shoulder and spoke over her head. "You, my dear, may be the one who will severe that bond."

Elizabeth felt his breath in her hair. She found it incomprehensible that he was not flesh and blood. He felt real. He even smelled real. His grip was like steel. He radiated tension and heat, like the time he'd made love to her.

He seemed to gather her close and hold her at every opportunity. She no longer thought it was endearing. She jerked out of his embrace. "Leave me out of it, Duncan. You're not going to drag me into this macabre game you and Angus are playing."

She left the couch and curled, facing him, on the floor across the room where she could watch his face while he spoke. The fire burning at her side made her feel queasy and overheated. She was about to learn a hurtful truth. He had known this moment would come from the first instant he knocked on her door. She could see it in his eyes. They were almost black with anticipation. She could try to stop him, but had never been able to dissuade him once he set his mind to anything. And she knew she wouldn't stop him if she could. Dread was a compelling, living thing in her stomach. She had to know.

"Angus and I are from the same town in Scotland. The source of our eternal friction lies in Scottish history,"

Duncan said. "I've a tale to tell. It's vital that you listen with an open mind."

"An open mind? I believe there are two ghosts in my house, toying with me, bedeviling me until I'm about to go crazy. Wouldn't you say that's open-minded?"

Duncan stood. "Perhaps this isn't the right time to tell you. You should go away for a while. Get out of this house and away from Angus. Prepare to listen to me without anger or judgment. Then I will return."

She pushed to her feet. "I'm not going anywhere. And neither are you! I want to know what's going on. I want to know now. If you don't tell me, I will-I will-"

"You will what? You have no power to make me do anything, you foolish girl."

It was as though he had slapped her. An intense wave of malevolence washed over her with such force she recoiled.

"That's not me. And it isn't meant towards you." Their eyes locked. "You can't stay here, Elizabeth. I know you won't leave unless I convince you."

Convince her of what? That the malice that gripped her radiated from Angus? Duncan had never spoken of her leaving before. He did want this house. He wanted to drive her away. He wanted to drive Angus away. "I felt safe here, before you came," she said.

"You were never safe. From the moment you entered this house you were in grave peril. Now you demand to know what's going on. I tried to tell you before. You didn't want to listen. You're ready to listen now, aren't you? So, be it."

So, be it. She wanted to put her hands over her ears. She wanted to run away. To not face what was coming. He was going to tell her things she didn't want to know about her beloved Angus--about her wonderful home. Her life would never be the same again.

Chapter **19**

"After the battle of Culloden," Duncan began, "life in Scotland began to change. The small, time-honored profits from renting to the peasants were negligible compared to the new fortunes to be made raising and grazing sheep. The feudal system had run its course. Peasant tenants, upon which the wealth of Scotland had been built over centuries, became obstacles in the way of progress. They occupied valuable land and had to be eliminated.

"Scottish landlords began to evict their tenant Highlanders so they could sell or lease the land to sheep farming operations. Years of persecution began.

"As you can imagine, those families who had lived there for generations didn't go easy. There was no place to go. The tenants were miserably poor. Many were old and ill. Few had skills with which to sustain their lives anywhere else.

"Those who wouldn't or couldn't leave were beaten, burned out and murdered. Many were captured and sold as slaves. It was part of an insidious scheme to empty the glens of human habitation."

Elizabeth had seen movies and read books about the battle of Culloden. "That was over two hundred and fifty years ago." He was speaking about a place and time so far removed it seemed irrelevant to her.

"The clearances began after Culloden, but they didn't happen overnight. The brutal atrocities lasted over one hundred years and almost totally eliminated a race of Celtic peoples before the Highlands were finally cleared."

"That's ancient history, Duncan. It's horrifying. But I hardly think it has anything at all to do with me."

"This is about Angus."

"And you?"

"And me."

"Were you a Highlander, Duncan?"

"I was, lass."

The burr of his accent, so new and unaffected, made her heart quicken with the sure knowledge he was indeed a spirit from the past and no mortal man.

"I was born towards the end of the misery. I came

from a good family that was sold out by our benefactors for fancy goods and a lavish lifestyle. My kin were brutalized and enslaved."

Elizabeth found she was no longer afraid. She wanted to sympathize with Duncan, but kept quiet so she wouldn't break his concentration.

"Angus and I are from Strathcarron, an area like many others, denuded of Scotsmen by Scotsmen for the sake of the profit to be made from grazing sheep."

"Strathcarron. So, Angus was a Highlander, too."

"Angus was a proctor in the service of the landowners."

"A proctor? Meaning he did their dirty work?" No wonder the animosity between Angus and Duncan was so palpable.

"Aye. Filthy, abhorrent work it was." Duncan's voice deepened with pain. "When the landlord of Strathcarron decided it was time to evict all of the remaining tenants, he sent in Angus and his thugs.

"Most of the townsmen were away in service to the Crown. The women resisted the order to abandon their homes and land. The constables were called in. The women stood fast, their children by their sides. I saw Angus give the order to knock them down with no mercy. The police struck with brutal force. They savagely beat the women and their children, killing some, mangling others."

Elizabeth could almost see the bloodbath. She could almost hear the cries and moans of those unprotected women and children. "You said most of the men were in the army, Duncan. Yet you were there." She tried to keep any note of censure from her voice.

"I was. I fought with all my strength, but I was attacked by three men and beaten unconscious. When I awoke, only the dead and dying remained. I found out soon enough the rest had been imprisoned.

"When I finally gathered enough strength to move, I dragged myself over the blood-soaked ground. I found my sister lying in a ditch, her face in the dirt, her hair torn from her scalp. She was dead, and so was the child she had been about to bear."

It happened over a hundred and fifty years ago, still the horror of it made Elizabeth mute.

"I went to my knees over my sister's body and raised my eyes to heaven, swearing vengeance." Duncan shimmered before her eyes with emotions so strong they disrupted his physical force. "I felt like I, too, died that day."

Elizabeth cried as if she had been there. She cried for the people of Strathcarron. She cried for Duncan. She cried for his sister and her baby. Long moments passed while she tried to come to terms with his story. "What about the rest of your family?" she finally managed.

"My parents had died the previous year. My two brothers died when they were wee bairns."

"I'm so sorry."

"Don't be. They all died natural deaths. If they had

lived, they would have suffered immeasurable pain and sorrow. It was a comfort to me at the time they had already passed."

Still, to go through so much and have no one to turn to must have been hell. "How did Angus wind up here, in America?"

"He knew he had to leave Strathcarron," Duncan said, "before the news of the atrocities made it to the menfolk. He took his blood money and left his guilt behind, abandoning his own family and his country.

"Angus fled Scotland on an immigrant ship, pretending to be one of the refugees. They sailed to Nova Scotia. The ship broke out with cholera. Passengers died like poisoned rats, their bodies thrown overboard with no burial rights and no records kept."

The circumstances were hard to imagine. Again, Elizabeth felt disconnected from the past.

"Over four hundred souls left Scotland on that ship. Those that lived were detained aboard the ship in Pictou Harbor until there was no more chance for the scourge to spread.

"Angus, the least deserving of them all, had boarded the ship in good health. He fared better than his starved and dispirited brethren. He was one of only one hundred and twenty left alive who were finally allowed to disembark.

"The refugees settled in Abercrombie, but Angus left Nova Scotia and immigrated to America. He flourished here, as you are aware."

"You followed him, didn't you? Were you on that ship, too?"

"I followed him, yes. But no, I wasn't on that ship."

"Why, with all the hatred between you, did you come here, to where he settled?"

"There was nothing to keep me in Scotland. Angus had ordered the massacre that destroyed my village. He took what I'd been entrusted with by the men with whom I'd grown up. He stole the future of Strathcarron and took the only woman I had left in the world to love. I have done my best, since the year of our Lord, eighteen fifty-four, to reciprocate."

Her pity evaporated. Was he saying because Angus loved her he was going to harm her? Or worse? She edged away from the fire, pushing a few inches father away from him.

He apparently didn't notice. His gaze remained on the far wall as if he were visualizing the horrors of the past.

"Why were you not serving the Crown with the other men of Strathcarron, Duncan? Why were you at home?" Somehow this seemed important to her. Maybe she had to know the worst about him so it would give credence to her fears. Was he a deserter? A coward? A criminal the army refused to accept?

"I was a minister," he choked. "It was my duty to take care of the spiritual and corporeal needs of my flock. I was supposed to keep them safe. I couldn't even keep my own sister safe."

Duncan, a minister? "Oh, Duncan, you were a man of God? Why didn't you tell me? How very guilty you must feel. You have to believe it wasn't your fault."

"I never said it was my fault." His accent was gone, his burr had softened into the low, soothing tone she'd come to think of as his voice. "I did the best I could. The fault lies with that spawn of Satan."

"Enough!" Her head was spinning. She felt ill. She refused to believe Angus was the villain Duncan described.

She certainly didn't agree with Angus's conception of Duncan. There had to be a mistake, a misunderstanding.

She would keep her skepticism to herself because she was uneasy with Duncan's sworn vengeance against Angus. She had no desire to become a pawn in their ghastly duel. "You have to leave, Duncan." She pushed to her feet. "Angela will be here any moment." In truth, she hadn't heard from Angela, even after her threat to return if she didn't show up at work.

"I'm not finished, my dear," he said. "There is so much more to tell you. So much more to explain. You need to be told, and you need to understand the rest."

"Not now. Please, just leave."

"Are you sure?" he asked. He rose from the couch and approached her.

"I'm sure." She flinched when he drew his fingers down her cheek in an intimate gesture. It was one thing to enjoy his caress when she thought he was mortal. She didn't know how she felt about him now, but she knew she didn't want him to touch her. Not yet.

"I'll leave you for now, but I will be back. You have to hear the entire story. Your life depends on it."

She almost shoved him out the door. She stared after him as he walked beyond the cedars. Where was he going? Had he ever stayed at the Lighthouse Inn?

Chapter **20**

The sun glowed pink through the windows on the west side of the living room. Another day had passed. Elizabeth still hadn't left the house.

She locked the door, turned out the lights and went upstairs. She stood hugging herself and staring at the bed where she and Angus had made love. It was, most likely, if she were to believe Duncan, the same bed where Angus had made love to Elizabeth Grayson. She had to know the truth before she lost her mind. "Angus!"

"I'm here."

"Where in hell have you been?" She'd never spoken

to him with such anger.

"I've been right here. You're not receptive to me anymore," he accused. "You want the truth? Here it is. Duncan killed his own sister. It was his child she carried."

Elizabeth cringed. What a horrible, disgusting accusation.

"Duncan lied about what happened that day. I didn't order the death of the Strathcarron women. I came too late to save them, but not too late to witness him bludgeon his sister to death."

"No!" she cried. "You're lying. Why would he kill his own sister? He loved her."

"She didn't love him. She hated and feared him, just the way he taught her. But she came to me for protection and had learned to love and trust me. I wanted to die the day she told me she carried his child. I loved her with my whole being, and took her as my lover and my betrothed when it was too late for me to father her child. I would have been a good husband. I would have raised the child as mine.

"He found out about us," Angus said. "He learned I had exposed his crimes against her. The landlord had promised leniency. It was Duncan who persuaded him to order the deadly attack against the town folk to camouflage his own sins. I had nothing to do with it. He carried his own torch that day and personally fired the hovels that provided the only sanctuary for the poorest of them. He left the sick and elderly inside their shelters. I can still hear their screams as they roasted to death."

She clamped her hands over her ears. Her brain resonated with those screams as if she too had heard them.

"I was there, I saw it all. The town was an inferno. The air was filled with cries for mercy. Bloody, broken bodies of women and children littered the streets. I was one man, powerless against the brute force of those in charge.

"My love and fear for Duncan's sister gave me strength to battle my way through the chaos. I was clubbed and beaten, but I made my way to her home. It was on fire. Before I could get to the door, it collapsed. I was certain she was inside. In my terror and grief I turned away.

"There she was, beyond the house, near a pile of rocks that marked the town well. I can still see her in that moment as if she were a painting in my mind. The braid she always wore had come loose. Her dress was in shreds and her thin legs looked like pale birch branches. Embers rained down around her. I cried out her name.

"She cried out, too. But it wasn't for me. 'No!' I heard just that one desperate word as she raised her arms, crossing them in front of her face. Duncan smashed one of those rocks down on her head. She staggered. There was a sharp crack as the second blow sent her to her knees. He fell on her, striking her with the rock several more times. Then he leapt to his feet and turned to me.

"I recognized him. He recognized me.

"He dropped the rock, red with her blood, and walked away. He was in no hurry. He knew I wouldn't follow. I fell to the ground and took her in my arms. She was already dead but I couldn't leave her. Believe me, sweetheart. I swear on my love for you, the evil one here is Duncan."

"He loves no one!"

"Duncan?" She spun at the sound of his harsh and bitter voice. He was there, behind her.

"In the eternal battle between Good and Evil, which one wins, Elizabeth?" Duncan asked.

"No!" she choked. "This is my home. You can't just appear whenever you want. You can't!"

"I can. If I believe it is necessary. Good always triumphs. Always," Duncan said. "Anything else is unthinkable. Look at me. I can manifest in human form because I am more powerful than Angus. My substance grows with each passing year. Angus cannot solidify. He is weak because I have righteousness behind my power."

A mist formed beside Duncan. The swirling cloud took on the features of a young, hard-bodied, hard-faced man with long dark hair. His eyes were black. His mouth was angry. Elizabeth gaped at her first vision of Angus.

"Do not believe him. He lies."

"Ask Angus why he was there in Strathcarron that day, Elizabeth."

"I was recuperating from battle injuries," Angus said. "I had returned home to find my beloved carrying his seed. I told the town what she was afraid to. I exposed his sin; and he was ostracized by the people he'd lived among since birth."

"He is a liar," Duncan said. "He speaks with the authority of Satan--the Devil and his hatred for all women."

Duncan slid his hand around Elizabeth's neck in a gentle, threatening caress. "He is working for his master, Elizabeth. He is after your eternal soul."

Her skin quivered where he touched her. "What was your sister's name, Duncan?"

"You already know."

"Of course. It was Elizabeth, too. Just like Elizabeth Grayson." Was there some truth in Duncan's terrible tale of the Elizabeths? Her heart bled for the tragic deaths of those two long ago women, one pregnant, one with a newborn baby. "Was Andrew's wife really the immoral woman you made her out to be? Did she cheat on her husband and seduce Angus?"

"She was exactly as I made her out to be. She was a sweet child, but matured into a wicked woman. I expected nothing less. Blood will tell."

Elizabeth put her fist to her mouth. "You—you were Andrew Grayson! You brought that Elizabeth over from Scotland, didn't you? Why?"

Duncan shot Angus a look of triumph. "Yes, I was Andrew Grayson. I married her in eighteen seventy-two and brought her here, to America. I married her to protect her from Angus."

"That makes no sense. Why would a woman in

Scotland be in danger from Angus?"

"He wanted her. He made several trips back to Strathcarron, looking for her. He never found her, but he would have."

"Looking for her in Strathcarron? What are you saying?" It took a moment, but when the idea struck, it burst with clarity. "The baby! She didn't die with her mother?"

"No. She didn't die, She was born in that ditch from a mother gone cold. Angus testified she had been murdered at the moment of her birth. He lied." Duncan pointed at Angus. "With all the clearances going on in the Highlands, the happenings that day would have passed. But his account of the death of that baby shocked even the most cold hearted of men."

"What happened to her?"

"She was raised in poverty and squalor by a crofter who also lost his home that day," Duncan said. "He went to the coast to live in a shack by the sea where he was told he could work at harvesting seaweed. But there was little market for it, and his family barely survived. He was a blessed man to have taken a mewling babe when he could barely support his own. He knew Angus was after her, yet the crofter kept her safe until she was grown."

"But she was your sister's child. You took your own niece for your wife?" She couldn't keep the disdain from her voice.

Duncan picked up on it. "Don't judge me so harshly. I

told you, I was a minister. I was a man of God who refrained from carnal knowledge of women."

She didn't want to think Duncan might have taken his own daughter as a man takes a wife. It was too farfetched and unspeakable. "Did she know she was your niece?"

She wasn't surprised Duncan didn't answer. No woman would willingly wed her uncle. No sane uncle would want his niece for his wife. How did marrying her save her from Angus? And why would Angus want her? "If you told the truth and Angus ordered that terrible attack on your sister and the town, why would he want her child?"

"He wanted to possess his daughter the way he had my sister."

His daughter? If Angus was betrothed to Duncan's sister it could be possible, but he said the child was conceived before her mother became his lover. Why, Elizabeth wondered, would he not claim his own child?

Angus had been Elizabeth Grayson's lover. It was repugnant enough to know he had carnal knowledge of both her and her mother, but that her ghost lover would commit incest was something she couldn't fathom.

That poor, innocent baby, claimed by both men to be fathered by the other. She had been abandoned as a child to a life of misery and poverty, yet they competed for control of her when she became a woman.

Had she suspected either her lover or her husband was her father?

Elizabeth suddenly knew with certainty she was descended from the poor pregnant woman who lost her life in that ditch in Strathcarron. She was descended from her child. Whoever the father of that baby was, she had his blood flowing in her veins, too.

One of her ghostly lovers was her far-removed grandfather. She screamed in denial and revulsion. "Get out, both of you. Leave me alone."

Duncan shot Angus a look of pure hatred.

"Don't say another word, Duncan," she cried. "Not another word. I won't listen. You can't convince me of anything right now. Neither of you can."

Angus shimmered; his image dimmed and began to fade. She reached for him, wanting to touch what she had seen. Before her hands met the translucent impression it dissipated.

Satisfaction curved Duncan's mouth before he stormed down the hall towards the front door.

He had appeared out of thin air, and now he left like a man. Was he trying to impress her with just how insubstantial Angus was, and how human he could be?

"Wait," she cried. "If you are really Andrew, why is your name now Duncan Munroe?"

But he was gone. They were both gone, and she was blessedly alone.

Elizabeth exhaled with a rush of air that ended in a sob. She felt like she had been punched in the heart. She couldn't stand there any longer, listening to the clock chime out the quarter hours. She had to move. She had to go to bed. She would force her mind to go blank. She would take a couple of sleeping pills and hide under her covers until they took effect.

"You have some control over him, it seems," Angus said, making her jump.

"I thought you had gone." She could barely keep the anger and disappointment from her voice. "I asked both of you to leave."

"This is my home, Elizabeth. I only leave if I choose."

"Really? And you choose to quite often, don't you?" she accused. "It seems like those times I need you are when you decide to be absent. And when I want you gone, you remain." All this time she had thought him to care more for her than any of her living lovers had. For the first time, she realized his behavior bordered on abusive control.

"I'm never absent. I am here with you at every moment. You are never alone."

Never? There were times when she, like every human being, needed privacy. She had always felt comfortable with Angus as a cohabiter, but this was sinister and disturbing. "So you stalk me?" Her laugh was a short huff of air that she caught with her hand across her mouth. "I've called for you, yet you didn't let me know you were there. I've needed you, needed the comfort and security of your presence, but you withheld that from me. I needed you to defend yourself against Duncan's accusations, but you chose to let me face them alone. Yet you say you're with me constantly? You're a cold-hearted bastard, Angus."

"Bastard I am not. Nor am I coldhearted. The fire within me is beyond earthly love. Beyond anything a living human can conceive of. You have not yet begun to experience it."

The mix of pleasure and pain, anticipation and fear he had already bestowed upon her was almost more love than she could bear. She shuddered at the thought of something horrifyingly beyond love.

She had to take some control immediately. She was no longer the submissive girl she used to be. "I've welcomed your presence, Angus. I've grown to love you. But you can't disregard that the way I live and feel is dictated by the fact I am alive.

"You were once. You must remember people who live together have to have rules and boundaries. This house may have been yours when you were alive, but it's mine now. My house, Angus, and I'm setting the rules from now on."

A feather light touch flitted up her spine then blossomed into an effervescent tingling that brought back the same sensations she had before losing consciousness in the bathtub.

"You do that, my dear."

She sank to her knees. Her eyelids drifted shut. Something wicked deep within her acknowledged she would welcome the near death passion again. Anything to blank out the dreadfulness, even if only momentarily.

And so she learned yet one more thing about herself.

But Angus withdrew and her lust bled into the floor, leaving her unbalanced. She sat on the rug with her face in her hands and wished she could snap her fingers and make Angus disappear.

"When Duncan comes to bedevil me, he materializes in different forms under different names," Angus said.

Her head reeled with the sudden change of subject. So he was going to dismiss her distress as if it meant nothing? She had never guarded her thoughts from him, but she knew now there were times he wasn't aware of what she was thinking. If she could keep her thoughts from him now perhaps she wouldn't feel so manipulated.

She stood and firmed her spine. "His name is Duncan, now," she said. "And he was once Andrew. What was his name in Strathcarron?"

"It doesn't matter. The fool believes he can deceive me," Angus said. "He did, once, when he had crossed and I was still mortal, but now we are on common ground and I always know who he is."

"When he had crossed? And you were still alive? But, he—he—killed you. You died first."

"You think so? I testified against him in Scotland. His crimes were terrible, but the elders were swayed most by the death of the baby. He was hung for the atrocities he committed in Strathcarron. His death was long and hard, as he deserved."

"Hung? He died in Scotland?" The shock of imagining Duncan hanging from a gallows, his arms bound, and his feet kicking made her want to throw up. This was worse than the mental image of Angus lying in a pool of blood on her kitchen floor. "But he said he followed you to America. Are you telling me his ghost followed you here? His ghost married Elizabeth, and shot you?"

"Aye."

The three of them, Angus, Andrew and Elizabeth had been responsible for each other's death.

Chapter **21**

Elizabeth couldn't bring herself to touch the diary. Duncan had been adamant that she read it. Why? Surely, he must think it would serve his purposes.

She was afraid of the diary, but knew eventually she would read it. She had to know the truth. She ruthlessly shoved away the suspicion she wanted the truth only if it exonerated Angus. What little she'd read of it certainly wouldn't do that. The passages had made Angus seem like a monster, a man with a broken mind.

But Angus, too, had wanted her to read it. Was he testing her loyalty? Trying to shock her?

She searched her home for any other clues to the truth, not knowing exactly what she was looking for. She found a box in a corner of the attic she'd never before investigated. It held loose pictures, brittle postcards and ledgers.

Some of the pictures were fairly recent. She found one of her aunt Marguerite and uncle Jasper. She touched their faces. She could hardly believe they were dead. She set the picture aside to be framed. The rest were decades old. The grainy sepia photographs were unmarked. In any case, they were all of a period after the time Angus, Andrew and Elizabeth would have lived. And the ledgers held no answers.

Her disappointment was strong. She wanted to see them. She wanted to connect the story to faces.

She carefully repacked the box. The final few pictures were of five young women in a garden. There was no date, but she guessed they were taken in the 1920's. Was one of the lovely women with her old-fashioned clothing and hairstyle her ancestor? She studied the faces, comparing them to the picture of her aunt Marguerite, and looking for something familiar to her own reflection.

She put the top on the box and set it aside to be gone through again someday. It held no answers to the story, but it held her history.

A log shifted and cracked, sending a shower of sparks snapping before falling, cool and dark and useless onto the hearth. The unceasing seas failed to muffle the sounds of shutters banging against the stone walls.

Spooky, that's what it was, spooky and bleak. Since Angus and Duncan had left, she'd come to see her home through Duncan's eyes. He was right. It was void of all the good things life held. It felt the way it had been when she'd first walked through the front door.

Only Angus and the happiness he inspired in her had kept the desolation at bay.

She realized she was lonely for the first time in years. She hadn't heard from Angela, or anyone for that matter. Even her mother had stopped writing. She would call them all tomorrow.

It was past time to approach Mr. Clark about her position. She wouldn't blame him if he had filled it with someone else. She needed her friends and her job. She missed her mother. She had always missed her, she realized. She had to put an end to this self-imposed exile before she lost everyone dear to her.

But she knew if she could rebuild her old life, it still wouldn't be enough to soothe her bone-deep loneliness. She was miserable. Life held no more joy or satisfaction.

This was how it would be if Angus and Duncan stayed gone forever.

The things of which they accused each other were depraved and abhorrent. Whether Duncan told the truth, or Angus told the truth, the baby Elizabeth, born of a dead mother, seemed to be a catalyst for an eternal battle between the two spirits.

The more she dwelled on their terrible tale, the less she believed it. As in all conflicts, a sense of righteousness usually spurred exaggerated accusations. Perhaps some parts of their story were true, but so much of it seemed beyond comprehension. Her heart rejected Duncan's allegations. Her mind did, too because anything else was a path to madness.

She was determined to forget every suspicion and evil accusation Duncan had planted in her mind. She knew Angus and loved him.

She didn't know Duncan well at all. At times he had displayed behavior that made her question his sanity. But that, she admitted, was before she knew his history. Before she found out he was no more alive than Angus. The truth was, Duncan stirred a desire in her she was helpless to control. She simply could not believe Duncan was the monster Angus claimed.

The realization she needed both of them almost brought a cry of protest. What kind of horrible woman was she?

Suddenly the house, as huge as it was, suffocated her. She had to get out in the fresh air.

Winter had been brutal and had brought its frigid weather into April. It seemed like spring would never come. Most of the snow had melted, leaving a thin film that had iced over last night. The sun was painfully brilliant. There was no wind.

Elizabeth went to the edge of the cliff and looked down, wondering from where Elizabeth Grayson had jumped. Where she had landed? She peered down the distance, almost expecting to see blood on the boulders below.

An indentation in the earth led to the steep, craggy path that fell almost straight to the beach below. In summer, she often worked her way down the incline to the isolated beach of black sand that wound in paths around scattered boulders. It always took great effort to climb down, and then back up, searching blindly with her feet for toeholds, grasping ancient vines and dead tree roots for leverage.

The path was slicked over with ice today. It would be suicidal to attempt to traverse it, but the sea's sounds were a siren song calling her to the beach. She couldn't get Elizabeth Grayson's tragic death out of her mind. She had a need to go to where the poor woman's spirit had parted with her body and pray for her soul.

Elizabeth took off her gloves and tossed them on the ground. Carefully she turned her back to the cliff and let her leg drop down to the first jutting rock. Then she slid her other leg over. Within minutes she had lowered herself beneath the promontory and could no longer see the safety of her lawn.

She pressed her body to the earth, and her face to the wall of the incline. Rocks, frozen dirt and crystallized lichen scratched her cheeks. This must have been what

Duncan's sister saw as she lay dying in that ditch in
Scotland.

Her fingers, numb from the cold, could barely feel the
roots and stones she grasped. The natural rock steps
formed so long ago by pounding water were slippery. She
concentrated on touching each step with her toe before
settling her weight on it.

Her boot slid off one, dropping her with no warning.
She screamed and tightened her curling fingers on the wall
of dirt. The fall ended with a thud as her other foot caught.
She waited, pressing her body against the stony surface
until her heart slowed down. Then she carefully began
descending again.

It took a long time to navigate the torturous path. She
finally reached the bottom and collapsed on the beach. Her
arms trembled uncontrollably. Her thigh muscles burned.
She sat with her legs tucked beneath her until her knees
began to ache. Stretching her legs in front of her, she
rubbed against cramps that intensified by the minute.

She lost track of time. But the tide did not. When cold
water lapped at her legs and seeped through her slacks it
numbed the cramps. She rose to her feet with the slow care
of an aged woman. Waves crashed, and then slid away,
nibbling at her boots. Sand shifted fluidly beneath her feet.
Her pant legs were wet and heavy. Ice formed thin
shackles around her ankles.

She'd never been so utterly alone. Time had no
meaning. She could have been standing there for a few

minutes, or for hours. Her mind was completely empty of worry, doubt and fear.

The emotional void brought with it a great weariness. She imagined sinking back to the ground and lying upon the obsidian sand until the tide covered her. She imagined being caught in the angry waves and rolling and tumbling out to sea. Perhaps it wouldn't matter one bit if the frigid, salty water filled her lungs.

Her hair whipped in her face, stinging her eyes. Her body ached from cold. The pain brought her out of her morbid trance. Sorrow and fear resurfaced with a vengeance. Tears ran down her face as she stared at the ocean. Where out there was Scotland?

A movement caught her attention. Something floated just beyond her reach. Each wave brought it closer and closer. She managed to snag it with her numb fingers. It was a length of cloth, a fragile yellow strip that came apart in her hands.

A rogue surge viciously sucked the sand from beneath her boots, threatening to topple her. This was dangerous and foolhardy. The tide was coming in. The wind was churning up. She flung the slimy gauze back into the roiling waters. She had to get back up to safety.

She looked to the shore. A man was there, not twenty feet away. *Duncan.* She pressed her fist to her mouth to stifle her scream.

He closed the distance between them so swiftly there was no time to react. He swept her into his arms. His expression was cold and cunning.

"Put me down," she cried.

"I will not let him have you."

Elizabeth struggled against his iron grip. "You're mad. Let me go!"

His eyes were dark and hard. "I cannot. He will steal your soul and hand it to the Devil. Trust me, Elizabeth. I will save you from eternal damnation." He turned to the sea and walked into the surf.

The last thing she saw before she fainted was the swath of shredded yellow fabric clinging to a rock as the sea viciously tried to reclaim it.

Chapter **22**

Elizabeth awoke to the scent of roses. A golden haze burned through her lids. She stretched, yawned and opened her eyes. The sun lit her room with a peachy glow and gave her a sense of well-being. Her heart told her Angus was with her.

She swung her legs over the side of the bed and sat there, her legs hanging down, her bare feet peeking out from under a nightgown she had never seen before. It was virginal white, high-necked and long-sleeved. The tiny pleats on the bodice looked hand sewn. She ran her hands over her arms. The material was soft and fluid and felt like satin.

"Angus?"

"I'm here."

Memory returned. The terror she'd felt in Duncan's arms came rushing back. "What happened? Where's Duncan? How did I get here?"

"I brought you here, sweetheart. I bathed you and dressed you. You have been asleep for two days."

"Two days? What happened to Duncan?"

"Duncan was going to kill you."

"No!" she cried. But she couldn't deny she had expected to die down there in the water. She'd felt Duncan's wrath and determination and had fully expected to be murdered.

"Yes, sweetheart, he intended to drown you. If he had succeeded you would belong to him forever. I stopped him."

"How, Angus?" She started sobbing. "How did you stop him from drowning me?"

"He is a cunning and powerful entity, but my love for you gave me the strength to wrest you from his clutches. You are now free from his evil intentions. You don't have to worry about him anymore."

What was he saying? Had he managed to make Duncan go away? Would she never see him again? A powerful desire to confront Duncan, with Angus's protection, coursed through her. What had she done to make him want to kill her?

Duncan had accused Angus of murdering the descendants of the first Elizabeth, but she now believed he had been responsible for their deaths. Apparently she was next on his list.

She shuddered, wishing once again Angus could hold her. "You appeared once, Angus. Can't you please come to me like Duncan did? I need to see you. I need you to hold me."

"That one time took all of my energy, Elizabeth."

Her name was spoken in a hissing whisper that reminded her of the sea. "Couldn't you try?" she begged.

"I cannot. I couldn't fully form then, and I know now I never will."

She climbed out of bed. Her fingers brushed the unfamiliar fabric when her arms fell to her sides. "Where did this nightgown come from?"

"It is my gift to you."

"But where did you get it?"

"It was Elizabeth Grayson's. She left it here the day she died."

She tore at the fabric, ripping it from her body and throwing it on the floor. "Why did you put this on me? I don't want to wear a dead woman's nightgown!"

"She only wore it once."

She stared at it. Revulsion turned to awe. Her many-times-removed grandmother had worn that very nightgown. She picked it up and closed her eyes, seeking a spiritual connection to the woman who was once flesh and blood. For an instant, she wished Elizabeth Grayson's ghost could join them.

"There is nothing left of her, my dear. Forget about her. Come with me." Angus's presence was a palpable thing, warm and comforting. It soothed her fears and made her believe he would protect her from all evil.

She dropped the nightgown and followed his voice as it led her onto the balcony. The frigid wind tore at her. Icy snow blew sideways, making tinkling sounds against the glass doors. It beat against her flesh, and yet she felt no cold.

"You and I are soul mates, Elizabeth," he said. "We are meant to spend eternity together."

"I know, my darling, I know." Her love became a fresh slate, washed free of every bad thing that had happened between them. Her heart knew Angus, and she trusted her heart. "Oh, Angus, I desperately want to see you. I want to touch you. I want to feel your touch. I wish we could be together in every way."

"I cannot return to earthly form like Duncan unless I, too, make a pact with Satan," Angus said. "We have each other, but we can never have what we truly desire."

Calm settled over her, along with the certainty her destiny had always been in her own hands. "You can't become mortal like me. But Angus, I can become like you."

"Yes, Elizabeth, you can. This thing you call life is only an interlude between where you came from and where you are going. It is a rare gift to be able to choose your destination."

Suddenly, Elizabeth knew nothing was impossible.

She could be with her ghostly lover for all eternity. It was her choice.

"You know what they will say?" Angus asked.

"I do. But they will be wrong."

"No!" The word came as a dull roar. "They will be right."

She whirled to the sound. "Duncan," she gasped, thoroughly shaken. He stood at the end of the balcony. Had he come from her bedroom? Had he had been there all along?

"Angus?" she cried. "You told me he was gone! You said you would protect me from him."

"I said you didn't have to worry about him anymore. You have the power to protect yourself, sweetheart."

"I can't protect myself. I need you! Are you abandoning me?" She put her fist to her mouth. She had wanted to confront Duncan, but now he terrified her.

"I would never abandon you, my love. Duncan cannot harm you without your consent. You have complete control over his impact on you."

"The decision you are about to make is vital to both of us, so in a way you have some control over both Angus and me," Duncan said. His voice turned low and compelling. "Don't be afraid of me, Elizabeth. I brought you here. I clothed you and put you in bed."

She shook her head in disbelief.

"It's true. I saved you. Angus was with you on the beach. He was in your mind. You were susceptible to his influence. If I hadn't come to you he would have persuaded you to drown. Your body would never have been found."

"I don't believe you."

"You won't admit you believe me, but you do. You know you would have killed yourself with no remorse, committing your soul to eternal damnation."

Duncan was wrong. But the seed of doubt had been planted. She remembered visualizing her body in the throes of the turbulent waters. She remembered thinking it would be a painless death if she chose to go that way. But, no, she had not been tempted. She was sure of it. "Angus?"

"There is no such thing as eternal damnation," Angus said.

"There is," Duncan said. "And there is redemption, the most precious gift of all. It was given to you before you were born, Elizabeth. You were about to throw it away. Close your eyes. Picture now what you imagined then. Can you see the tide flowing over your lifeless body? You were on the brink."

"Can you read my mind, too?" She wanted to weep. Her mind had been invaded. If they could steal her thoughts, could they plant them?

"I cannot sway you in any way," Duncan said. "But Angus has immense ability to do so. You have been caught up in the vortex of his mental domination. Elizabeth, please listen to me. You are our only hope of breaking this evil cycle. If you follow him, you will join the lost souls he has stolen. Let me help you stand strong against him."

"Nonsense," she cried. "I'm not controlled by him! He has never made me to do anything against my own will."

"Really? You should have gone to church that day, my dear."

Suddenly all the glacial torment of the weather broke into her consciousness. She shivered uncontrollably, crying out from the frigid pain. "Don't call me that!" She crossed her arms over her bare breasts and turned away from Duncan, ashamed to be naked while she was defending Angus. "I love him."

"I know you do. They all loved him. That is his weapon against me."

"But he didn't love them." She sounded pitiful to her own ears.

"True. He is incapable of love. He bartered that precious commodity away for a life of riches that lasted only until he shot himself."

"But--but you shot him!"

"I've never taken a life, Elizabeth. Angus has no reverence for life, even his own."

"He shot himself?" Of all the horrors Duncan had revealed, this was the worst. Had Angus deliberately ended his mortal life? Was he now trying to convince her to do the same so he wouldn't be alone in his ghastly existence?

But he wasn't alone. According to Duncan he was accompanied by the souls of the previous Elizabeths. A rage went through her at the thought of sharing Angus. She wished them all into hell and quickly blessed herself, knowing at that moment, her own soul was in jeopardy.

"You know he killed Angela," Duncan persisted.

"He did not murder Angela!" she screamed. "He didn't."

"He did. You became aware of that the moment you saw her scarf in the water."

"You lie! Angus had no reason to harm her." Angela couldn't be dead. She couldn't. She was going to have a baby.

"You would have confided in her eventually. He knew that."

"I would never betray Angus. I've never told a single soul about him."

"You told me."

"But that was only after—after--" she stuttered, suddenly confused. "But you already knew. Didn't you?"

"Read the diary, Elizabeth," Duncan pleaded. "Know the truth before you make this decision." He held the book in his hand. "Evil is a seductive lie. The truth is your only chance at redemption. This tells the complete story. Read it." He tossed the book to her.

She watched it fly past her without attempting to prevent it from sailing over the balustrade. She wouldn't listen to him or touch the diary. He was trying to destroy her relationship with Angus.

Her mind reached out to Angus.

He was waiting. His aura was vibrant with triumph. "You are familiar with the heavy hand of authoritarian men, my dear," he said. "It's time for you to make your own decision with no fear of repercussions."

The soothing balm of his adoration enveloped Elizabeth. He'd waited patiently for Duncan to make his case because he knew what her decision would be. He had never doubted her.

"Shall we take a stroll to the cliffs, sweetheart?" he asked.

She gave a sough of relief. "Yes!" A slightly hysterical laugh broke in her throat, almost choking her. Her hands clenched and unclenched in a need to grasp Angus.

Her elation turned to terror as Duncan began to shimmer with rage. His body pulsated and turned almost translucent.

Angus formed into a dervish of powdery, noxious disconnected matter that whirled around her. She gasped, inhaling and choking on soot she knew was formed of her ghost. He was inside her now--a part of the very breath of her. She imagined she could feel him being absorbed into her lungs, transported to her blood and rushing through her veins and arteries to her heart. Her core.

Duncan shouted in outrage. He leapt towards Angus—towards her. "It's not too late!" he screamed. "Choose life! Choose it now while you still can!"

The soot of which Angus was formed turned into cinders that fell all around her, striking her flesh with needle-like pricks and hitting the wood with tiny pings. Elizabeth cringed and slipped to the floor, ducking her head into her arms. She knew she was about to topple into the oblivion of unconsciousness.

"Just say, 'no', Elizabeth. Say, 'No', and I can save you," Duncan pleaded.

Her lips moved. Soft words escaped before she fainted.

Elizabeth found herself standing on the edge of the promontory. She had no recollection of how she got there, yet she knew Angus was beside her.

She looked back and saw Duncan had stayed on the balcony, far above them. His dark figure was dwarfed by the grotesque house. His long coat snapped in the wind. His arms were spread as if to beckon her to come back to him. She sensed his anguish.

If only she knew the reasons behind his attempts to wrest her from Angus. Why was it so vital to him that she read the diary? What did he want her to find out about her ghosts' terrible, entwined history? More than anything she wanted to know why she was so important to them.

"Elizabeth," Angus said. "Focus on me. You have made your decision."

"I have?"

"Duncan cannot stop you. He has no influence over your free will. Do you love me?"

214

She reached out as if to touch the sky. "I love you, Angus."

"I love you, Elizabeth. Are you ready?"

"Fool!" Duncan screamed.

Elizabeth looked behind her as she took the step that sent her spinning out into thin air. Duncan's face was distorted with rage and agony.

The presence of a woman with long chestnut hair and full red lips shimmered beside him. "*Amadian!*" she cried. "You made the wrong choice."

Caught by the wind, her words were scattered before Elizabeth struck the rocks below.

Epilogue

16 months later

The realtor looked around the living room, taking in the ornate moldings and high tin ceilings. Even the furniture was original to the period. Junk, she thought, impatient for the couple to finish their exploration. She didn't get the charm of old stuff. If she owned this house she would throw it all out.

She caught the swift movement of a shadow from the

corner of her eye. Mice! Or worse, rats.

The couple took their time wandering around upstairs while she waited down in the hallway beneath the ornate staircase. The wood was dark and carved with unrecognizable creatures with blank eyes.

She shivered. The August heat apparently didn't infiltrate the stone walls of this old place because the interior was as cold as a tomb. The surf boomed below the cliffs. Its sounds echoed through the rooms, taking the place of more familiar noises like traffic and children laughing.

Although the house was sound and quite beautiful in a Gothic way, in the realtor's opinion it was located too far from town. She was uncomfortable showing it. Perhaps she could persuade her clients to look elsewhere so they could get out of here.

The couple was halfway down the stairs when they lingered. The man hooked his arm around the woman's neck and drew her close for a kiss on the top of her head. The display of intimacy was almost like a private celebration.

The realtor turned her gaze away and announced, "I am bound by law to tell you there was a death on this property." A small sense of satisfaction coursed through her for interrupting their obvious peace. The sooner they lost interest in the property, the sooner they could leave.

"We know," the woman said as they descended to the entry hall. "Our waitress told us this morning when we mentioned we were interested in this place. It doesn't bother us."

"The owner was found dead on the beach below the promontory," the realtor continued. "They say it was suicide, but some think it may have been murder." She was certain telling the tragic tale would change their minds. Then she could take them to view the Tyler Mansion, a smaller Federal home within the town limits. It was as authentic and visually appealing as this house, but not so desolate.

"Please, don't say another word about it." The woman shuddered and gave a little grimace. "If we are going to live here, I'd rather not know." She stroked the mahogany door casing. Her expression turned dreamy. "That old hall tree is beautiful. And look at this gorgeous sideboard. You say the furniture comes with the house?"

"Yes. Everything in the house and on the property conveys. The realtor turned away, hiding her calculating expression. Was there a possibility she could actually sell this creepy place? "Would you like some time to talk it over; or perhaps you are ready to write an offer?"

"How do you feel about that, Chloe?" the man asked his wife.

"Oh yes, I'm ready. I love this house. I love this town." She turned to the realtor. "My ancestors lived in Midville. I have always felt I was destined to move here."

Her husband gave her an affectionate squeeze. "Maybe they lived in this very house."

"Wouldn't that be something? Oh, honey, I hope they accept what we can afford to offer."

The realtor smiled. "The county holds the deed for unpaid taxes. I'm certain they will accept any reasonable offer. You may even be able to move in before your baby is born."

"I hope so."

"Do you know if it's a boy or a girl?"

Chloe rubbed her stomach. "It's a girl. She's due on Christmas day."

The couple wandered into the living room.

The realtor followed, excited now by the possibility of a substantial commission.

Chloe touched the arm of an overstuffed chair. "I can see myself sitting here, nursing her by a warm fire."

"Have you chosen a name?"

"Not yet. We decided to wait until she is born." She gazed through the leaded windows to the sea beyond. "I think an old fashioned name will suit a child born in this lovely old home."

The couple walked outside, hand in hand, chattering enthusiastically about planting shrubs and painting walls.

The realtor stuffed her papers into her briefcase and hurried after them. She didn't want to be left alone in this mausoleum of a house.

She paused for a moment. *What was that noise?*

A special thanks to my readers!

I sincerely hope I have entertained you. If you enjoyed the book please pass the word and consider leaving a review. I appreciate all readers' comments and can be reached at sbrarey@aol.com.

Thank you

Sandra Brown Rarey

I am forever grateful for the patience of my husband of forever, and the guidance of two very special friends, Susan Weber and Sarah Parrott.

If you would like to read more about the Scottish Clearances go to: http://www.educationscotland.gov.uk/scotlandshistory/jacobitesenlightenmentclearances/clearances/

About the Author

Sandra Brown Rarey lives in a 140 year old farmhouse near the Chesapeake Bay with her husband, three cats, two dogs and assorted wildlife who share their chow.

Her fiction has won numerous awards including a National League of American Pen Women's award, The Writers Workshop award and Christopher Newport University's Maryanne Farley Award for Fiction. Her short stories and serialized fiction have been featured in a national publication with distribution to 4 million readers.

She loves hearing from her fans and can be found on facebook.com/sandrabrownrarey.

Her website is: http://srarey.bravehost.com

Coming soon:

THE CURSE

by

Sandra Brown Rarey

A young girl's pact with an evil entity leads to unforgivable acts that tear apart a Highland village.

Also by Sandra Brown Rarey

Book One:

Abraca-Uh-Oh!

What if the worst mistake you ever made turned out to be the best thing that ever happened to you?

Available on Amazon.com

Abraca-Uh-Oh!

What happens when a love spell goes terribly awry? Synthia Stone, owner of a shop of love spells called A Little Red Magic, finds out when she unwittingly sells her premium love spell to be used as a game at a wedding shower. During an evening of alcoholic revelry the guests collectively conjure a dream lover and then dump him off at A Little Red Magic. Synthia is stuck with the fantasy man none of the women want to claim. He has a dreamy voice and an infectious sense of humor, but he has margarita-inspired flaws and doesn't come close to being the man she has been dreaming of her whole life. She makes the mistake of taking him home and trying to fix him so she can pawn him off on someone else before her own Prince Charming comes into her life—if he ever shows up.

There's no way Red can be convinced he isn't a real, normal human with a slight amnesia problem. He is on a mission to discover who he is and needs the help of the irritable, messy, pixy-faced witch who seems to want to keep him a prisoner. He reacts to Synthia's attempts to alter his outrageous physical and mental characteristics with resistance as he changes her conception of the perfect man, and teaches her to believe in the magic in which she dabbles.

A Little Red Magic
Book One:
Abraca-Uh-Oh!

by
Sandra Brown Rarey

Poor Synthia Stone . . . her spells don't go quite as planned. The result is a laugh-out-loud romantic comedy that will have you rooting for the unlucky witch and believing, once again, that true love is the strongest magic of all.

> ~ Amazon review

Engaging characters. Bright, funny and entertaining!

> ~ Amazon review

The Ghost